"Brent?" Jen laid a hand on his arm, and his mouth went dry.

"What?" he croaked.

"Aren't you going to kiss me good night?"

Blood roared into his head. He wedged his fingers under the collar that had suddenly become two sizes too tight. "I don't . . . *ahem* . . . I don't think that's such a good idea," he choked out, and took another step in retreat.

"But—"

Jen bit her lower lip, and her gaze dropped to the floor. It hit him then that she *wanted* him to kiss her but was too shy to press the point.

"Sweetheart, I'd like nothing more than to kiss you right now."

"Well, then—"

"But," he interjected, laying a finger over her lips, "if I do that, I'm going to want to do a whole lot more. Do you understand? I want you too much to stop at a kiss tonight."

She reached up, curled her fingers around his wrist, and tugged his hand away from her mouth. Then she swallowed and took a deep, trembling breath. Looking him right in the eye, she whispered, "Okay."

She understood. Trying to ignore the swift, sharp stab of disappointment, he smiled crookedly. "Go on in now. Tomorrow we'll—"

"No." She moistened her lips. "I mean, okay, we'll do a whole lot more."

His stomach went into immediate free fall.

WHAT ARE *LOVESWEPT* ROMANCES?

They are stories of true romance and touching emotion. We believe those two very important ingredients are constants in our highly sensual and very believable stories in the LOVE-SWEPT line. Our goal is to give you, the reader, stories of consistently high quality that may sometimes make you laugh, sometimes make you cry, but are always fresh and creative and contain many delightful surprises within their pages.

Most romance fans read an enormous number of books. Those they truly love, they keep. Others may be traded with friends and soon forgotten. We hope that each LOVESWEPT romance will be a treasure—a "keeper." We will always try to publish

LOVE STORIES YOU'LL NEVER FORGET
BY AUTHORS YOU'LL ALWAYS REMEMBER

The Editors

FOR
LOVE OR
MONEY

KATHY
DiSANTO

BANTAM BOOKS
NEW YORK · TORONTO · LONDON · SYDNEY · AUCKLAND

FOR LOVE OR MONEY

A Bantam Book / August 1997

ISBN 0-553-44627-4

Published simultaneously in the United States and Canada

*Bantam Books are published by Bantam Books, a division of Bantam Dou-
bleday Dell Publishing Group, Inc. Its trademark, consisting of the words
"Bantam Books" and the portrayal of a rooster, is Registered in U.S.
Patent and Trademark Office and in other countries. Marca Registrada.
Bantam Books, 1540 Broadway, New York, New York 10036.*

PRINTED IN THE UNITED STATES OF AMERICA

OPM   0 9 8 7 6 5 4 3 2 1

To Mom, Vicki, and Grandma—
three California ladies
who have never let me down

ACKNOWLEDGMENTS

Gene Fowler once said, "Writing is easy. All you do is stare at a blank sheet of paper until drops of blood form on your forehead." He wasn't far off.

But if a writer is very lucky, she'll find a few good people who'll help make the process a little less painful. Good friends, like Donna Grove and Ginny Aiken, who will ease her through the rough spots. A good agent, like Linda Hyatt, who believes in her, gets in her corner, and cheers her on. A good editor, like Joy Abella, who'll—ever so gently, mind you—help a writer make her story better.

Thank you all.

PROLOGUE

Donnerton, California
June 1997

"Good God, he's doing it wrong." Jen reread the paragraph in disbelief. "Somebody should tell him."

"Who?" Candy's tanned thigh shifted languidly. She sounded as if she were almost asleep. Jen envied her. Tanning would be bearable if you were sleeping.

"Brent Maddox."

Candy's lips curved lazily. "Brent Maddox." The inflection said it all. "Honey, that man doesn't do *anything* wrong. Trust me."

"His love life's a mess."

One blue eye popped open to telegraph disbelief before closing again. "And Mother Teresa's a Libyan terrorist."

"Hey, this comes straight from the man himself. Listen. 'Marriage? Maybe someday, if I find a woman who's interested in me instead of my money. I haven't met anybody like that yet.'" She tossed her copy of *Celebrity* magazine onto the patio.

"Poor baby."

Jen eyed her bottle of suntan lotion, then sighed, settling back on her chaise. She would burn anyway. "If you ask me, he's got nobody but himself to blame."

"Hmm."

Eyes closed, Jen let the sun beat down on her. Sunbathing was one ritual she'd never gotten the hang of. Actually, it was doing nothing she'd never gotten the hang of; the work ethic was too deeply embedded in her DNA. "Think about it. If a man wants a woman to see past his money, he shouldn't whisk her off in his helicopter to a private mountaintop for lobster and champagne like Brent did to that poor model Daphne Carlson."

Candy groaned. "Oh, stop! Lobster. Dom Pérignon. Brent Maddox all to myself on a mountaintop. Talk about a fantasy!"

Small-town practical to the soles of her size fives, Jen would have called it ostentatious overkill. "Exactly. A fantasy. Brent sets himself up then whines about the results."

A chuckle bubbled up from Candy on the neighboring longue. "And *you're* going to set him straight? No offense, but the woman who spent her last date fighting off Bernie Wilkins at the Sundowner Drive-in isn't qualified to give Brent Maddox advice on his love life."

"It's not a matter of experience, it's a matter of common sense."

Candy shook her head. "No wonder you're as pure as the driven snow at twenty-eight. Common sense and romance don't go together. Now, *Brent Maddox* and romance—*they* go together."

Scowling, Jen placed her hands behind her head and mouthed Candy's words: *Pure as the drive snow.* And who's fault was that? she wondered. She certainly had her share of simmering female hormones. She just hadn't met a man who made them boil.

Mere chemistry was no reason to have sex. Making love should mean something. If an attitude like that made her a dinosaur, so be it. She might have antiquated notions, but they were *her* antiquated notions, and she didn't intend to defend them to anyone, including Candy.

"He needs a new approach. Like loading his date in a pickup with a bucket of fried chicken and a six-pack and driving to a national park. Any woman who still likes a man after a long drive, cold chicken, and warm beer is seriously smitten."

"Or desperate," murmured Candy.

"If a man doesn't want a woman lusting after his money, he shouldn't throw it in her face. I thought Brent had more sense."

"You say that like you know him."

"I do . . . or did. We went to high school together." A loud crash had her opening her eyes.

Candy gaped up from the patio, her chaise longue sprawled on its side behind her. "You know Brent Maddox?" Her voice rose half an octave. "You *know* him?"

"I *knew* Brent Maddox. It was a long time ago."

"Oh . . . my . . . God!" Hot-pink nails speared into a cap of platinum-blond hair. The fact that the hair color was natural didn't make Jen jealous anymore. Brown hair was nice, too. Boring, but nice. "What was he like?"

Jen shrugged carelessly. "Friendly. Cheerful but

cocky. I didn't know him that well—he was three years ahead of me." Which hadn't stopped her from joining the ranks of the anonymously besotted. "But he didn't have girl problems. God knows they were crawling all over him. And until that estate lawyer located the Maddoxes and notified them of their inheritance, he was as dirt-poor as the rest of us. You'd think he'd remember."

"He's living a different life now."

"Hmm. Well, I'm sure he'll manage." Dismissing the subject, Jen squinted toward the sun. It wasn't inclined to go down. "You know, I think I'll just get something to drink." And stay inside. And read a book.

Candy was right on Jen's heels. "I've got an idea."

Now, why would a simple statement like that make the back of her neck prickle? "What's that? You want some iced tea?" Jen opened the refrigerator.

"Yeah. Look, you said somebody should tell him."

"Tell who?" Standing on tiptoe, she snagged two glasses. Why didn't they build shorter cabinets for people who were five one?

Candy's knuckles rapped gently against Jen's head. "Hello? Pay attention here. You said somebody should tell Brent Maddox what he's doing wrong."

"Uh-huh." The neck prickle got pricklier. "So?"

"So," Candy crowed, "you be the one to tell him."

Jen's first swallow of tea went down the wrong way. A few sputtering seconds later: "I thought you said I wasn't qualified!"

"That was before I knew you and Brent were old friends."

Jen set the glass on the counter and gripped her

friend's shoulders so she could look her dead in the eye. "Listen. Brent and I went to the same high school, yes. He was the most popular boy in school. I was president of the Poetry Club. Maybe, *maybe* he said hello to me twice a year in the hallway. Do you understand what I'm saying here?"

Apparently not. "You can write him." Candy hurried away to the den, leaving Jen to follow.

"I don't know his address, and even if I did—"

"His address." Candy gnawed on her lower lip. "I know! You can send it care of *Celebrity*. They'll forward it." She sat and rummaged through the desk's top drawer.

"I am not going to write Brent Maddox with advice on his love life."

Candy popped up, paper and pen in hand. "Yes, you are."

Hands on hips, Jen stared at her. Was this the ultra-pragmatic girls' gym teacher she'd known and loved? How could you be colleagues and best friends with someone for two years and not know they were crazy? "Forget it." She was not going to get involved in this harebrained scheme. Not in a million years. Not on a bet.

"I dare you."

Uh-oh.

Jen had never been able to resist a dare. When she was five, Terry Sudman dared her to climb the towering oak in the Sudmans' front yard. The ascent hadn't been so bad, even though Jen's heart was in her mouth all the way up. Unfortunately, the trip down had been a lot quicker. She broke her right arm in the fall.

Just as memorable was the time her brother dared

her to prove she was immune to poison oak. She'd marched into the woods, plucked a handful, and scrubbed it over her arms and legs, only to spend the next two weeks crusty with Calamine lotion and having to answer to the sobriquet "Lizard Woman."

A person should learn from past mistakes. Nevertheless, a scant hour later Jen found herself staring into the gaping maw of the corner mailbox. *What on earth was she doing?*

She wiped one damp palm against her thigh. Her other hand clenched, mangling the envelope. "Maybe I should take this home and make a few changes. Yeah!" She beamed at Candy with desperate enthusiasm. "It would be even better then."

"You're trying to wimp out."

"But—"

"I double-dare you."

Jen opened her mouth on another attempt at reason.

"I *triple-dog-dare* you."

That did it. A triple-dog dare was a grave challenge. Her spine snapped straight. Ignoring the butterflies dive-bombing her stomach, Jen pasted on a devil-may-care smile and with a nonchalant flick of her wrist sailed the letter through the opening. "Hah!"

"Atta girl!" Candy rubbed her hands together. "Now all we have to do is wait for an answer." She turned and started back down the sidewalk. "I wonder how long it'll take?"

An answer. That wonderful, I-showed-her feeling died a quick death. Jen's gaze shifted from Candy's retreating back to the mailbox. Oh, boy. Turning slowly, she trailed after Candy, trying to convince herself she hadn't done anything really stupid. As usual, common sense came to her rescue.

There was no guarantee *Celebrity* would forward the letter. Even if they did, Brent Maddox was probably a very busy man, what with all that jet-setting and socializing. He had more exciting things to do than read mail from near-forgotten classmates.

Her step grew lighter. Heck, a personal secretary probably handled his mail. Brent wouldn't see the letter at all. Her sigh was one hundred percent relief. It was going to be all right. She was in the clear.

Celebrity magazine didn't forward Jen's letter: They printed it.

Dear Brent,

I can't help myself. It's a compulsion, this need to correct errors and educate others. No doubt it's the teacher in me, but when I saw the article about you in *Celebrity* magazine, I had to write. You're in desperate need of remedial instruction.

You know, Brent, you're the last person I'd expect to need this kind of tutoring. Back at Donnerton High, you were at the head of your class when it came to romance. Don't worry, I'm sure it will all come back to you with a little review.

All right, let's look at your situation logically. The attraction: Is it you, or your money? Fact number one: You're rich. Fact number two: There are women out there trolling for sugar daddies or wealthy husbands. Your problem, as I understand it, is how to avoid those less scrupulous women and find one who's genuinely interested in you. Simple. Stop thinking with your wallet!

Come on! Can you really expect a woman, even a "good" woman, to see you clearly when you throw luxury in her face? Personal helicopters? Private mountaintops? Gourmet picnics? My God, what are you doing to those poor women?

It's not like you need the props, is it? Twelve years ago all you had was a job busing tables at the Blue Anchor, a Harley, and an attitude, and you were knee-deep in blondes, brunettes, and redheads. If silly smiles and yearning sighs are anything to go by, you did fine without a penny to your name. (Mary Jane Sanders bumped into walls for a week after her date with you, and she preferred college men.)

So what's changed? Get back to basics! Ditch the copter and haul out the Harley!

You've lost a few points, Brent, but it's not too late to raise your grade. Don't force me to flunk you on this.

Sincerely,
Jennifer Casey

ONE

One month later

Nothing had changed.

The buildings strung along Main Street looked exactly the same, down to the last faded brick. Philbert's Pharmacy and Larson's Market stood shoulder to shoulder on the corner of Main and Auburn, windows plastered with handmade posters advertising everything from vintage Mustangs to bake sales. From the looks of the crowd, Queenie's, a combination drive-in and hangout, was still the place where boy met girl—only nowadays he met her in a higher class of car.

Calling Donnerton a one-horse town would be stretching it by a horse. Twelve years ago Brent Maddox had happily emigrated in a big way, thanks to three-times-removed cousin-by-marriage Graham's money. The only thing the eighteen-year-old had taken with him for Podunk was a strong aversion to coming back.

He was here only because he had a score to settle.

The forest-green Jag prowled down Main and swung right onto Grass Valley Lane, dragging curious stares in its wake. Brent cozied the car up next to the curb and killed the engine. Wrists draped over the steering wheel, he studied the white stucco house across the street. From its pristine black shutters to its neatly manicured lawn, 229 was an ordinary tract house.

No, it was the woman who *lived* in 229 that was an out-of-the-ordinary menace. He hadn't even remembered her until he dug out his old yearbook. But thanks to her letter, he'd had to face snickers on the tennis court and razzing at the marina. To the crowd at Spago he was a laughingstock, especially since Leno fired his latest salvo.

A man could only take so much flak before he gave in to the urge to dish some out.

Lips curving with grim relish, he opened the door and unfolded his six-foot-three-inch frame from the bucket seat. Raking a hand through his wavy blond hair, he crossed the street and strode up the walk.

What would Jen Casey say when she found him on her doorstep?

She screamed.

What woman wouldn't?

First of all, nobody likes to clean closets. But Jen was determined to bring order to the chaos behind doors number one, two, and three or die trying—a distinct possibility if all that junk fell on her. The rescue squad wouldn't find her body for days.

If looks could kill, her lime-green shorts and neon-pink T-shirt would slay them in droves. Most of her hair was bunched in a careless ponytail. Makeup hadn't rated a passing thought.

By late morning, she'd hauled everything out of the closets in her bedroom and the spare room, separating the contents into categories: Save and Put Back, Donate to Charity, and To Save or Not to Save. Good intentions aside, Trash was her smallest category.

She was on her knees in front of the treacherous hall-closet junk tower when the phone rang. "Oh, for—"

In the rush to answer, she jarred a strategically placed box and set the whole pile teetering. A strong sense of self-preservation had her slamming the door on the impending avalanche before she hurried into the living room. "Hello."

"Ohmygod, ohmygod, ohmygod!"

"Candy?"

"Ohmygod."

"Candy, what's wrong?"

"Ohmy—"

"God," Jen finished. "Candy, what in the world is going on? Are you all right?" Something was up; Candy wasn't prone to squealing and babbling.

"Have you seen it?"

"Seen what?"

"*Celebrity*. Have you seen the latest issue of *Celebrity*?"

"No, I—"

"It just came out. Well, actually, it came out about two weeks ago, but Philbert's didn't get their shipment right away—"

"Candy—"

"—because their supplier had trouble with a couple of his trucks and the deliveries got pushed—"

"Candy—"

"—back and I just happened to be standing there when they unloaded the—"

"*Candy!*"

"What?"

Enunciating carefully, Jen asked, "What is going on?"

"Ohmygod. They printed it! They printed it, Jen!"

She still didn't understand, but her neck was prickling like crazy. "What did they print?"

"Your letter! Can you believe it? They printed your letter!"

"Oh . . . my . . . God." Jen sat down on the floor. Hard.

"Isn't that great?"

"Great," Jen murmured faintly, and struggled to comprehend the scope of this latest disaster. *Celebrity magazine had printed her letter! "Ohmygod."*

"Yeah!"

Maybe she would be spared complete humiliation. "Did they leave out my name?" *Please, God.*

"Nope! They printed that, too! Big as life. Isn't that great?"

"Great?" Try as she might, she couldn't keep her voice from rising hysterically. "Great? Are you crazy? This is terrible!"

"Why?"

"Why?" Jen was rendered temporarily speechless. "Because . . . well, because . . . It just is, that's all."

"Oh, don't be such an old fuddy-duddy! You're

famous, Jen Casey, that's what you are! I can't wait to tell everybody."

"Candy, don't—" The line went dead. By the time Jen recovered her wits and hit redial, Candy's phone was busy.

"Wonderful. Just wonderful." She stomped down the hall and jerked open door number three. A tidal wave of junk buried her up to her knees.

By early evening the flood of calls and visits had ebbed.

Closet categories were strewn down the hallway and into the living room. Jen was sweaty and tired, her mood hovering between a groan and a snarl. With an absent shove at her wilted ponytail, she surveyed the damage and shook her head. Dynamite might be the answer.

Then some idiot rang the doorbell.

"Not again," she groaned, and waited. Maybe they'd go away. The bell pealed again. When the intruder pounded on the door, she gave up and threaded her way through the piles on the floor. Stepping in between Trash and To Save or Not to Save, more than ready to be rude, she gave another ineffectual push to her drooping hair, took a deep breath, and swung open the door.

"Jennifer? Jen Casey?"

The rolling baritone drew her gaze up the man's chest—and what a chest it was—to his tanned throat. On up to a chin chiseled with a faint cleft and a smile that could melt the cartilage in a woman's knees at forty paces. An awful dread unfurled in her stomach as Jen's eyes drifted helplessly upward to meet a pair as blue as a summer sky at twilight.

His wasn't a face a woman could forget, even after twelve long years. For one frozen moment horror held her motionless.

Then she screamed.

She shut the door in his face!

Brent's jaw dropped. It took him a couple seconds to realize it and close his mouth. His eyes narrowed. *She actually shut the door in his face!*

Women reacted to Brent Maddox. He was used to everything from giggles to longing sighs. They came onto him, both in public and in private. But having one scream, then slam a door on him was a novel experience. Insulting, but novel.

He hadn't even gotten a good look at her, dammit. All he had were impressions. A disheveled knot of brown hair, brown eyes wide with dismay dominating a pale face. And a banshee's shriek that made his ears ring.

Bending at the waist, he peered through the stained glass set in the door. She was braced defensively, back against the panel. Who did she think he was, for Christ's sake, the Boston Strangler?

He still couldn't believe it. She'd damn well shut the door in his face! His jaw flexed.

She wasn't going to get away with it.

"Jennifer?" He rapped on the glass and saw her jump. "Jen? It's Brent, Brent Maddox. I've come a long way to see you. Can I come in?"

Her head thunked back against the glass with a groan. "Oh, God."

"I just want to talk to you." Still no response. "Listen, Jennifer, you might as well let me in. I didn't drive three hours to talk to a door. I'm tired and hungry and cranky as hell, and I'll stand here all night if I have to. You've caused me a lot of trouble, lady. Now open up!"

She straightened slowly. Squaring her shoulders, she turned. The door swung open, and he was greeted with the phoniest smile this side of Hollywood. "Hello, Brent."

"Hello, Jennifer," he drawled, lips twitching. Her breezy greeting didn't quite come off; if her face got any redder, her head would combust.

"What . . . uh . . ." Her eyes darted away, then—unwillingly, he was sure—slid back to meet his. She moistened her lips, drawing his attention to her mouth. He blinked. Jennifer Casey had a great mouth—full, a little pouty. Quite a contrast to the button nose. "What are you doing here?"

His gaze lifted to those Bambi-brown eyes, and he smiled like a shark. "I got your letter."

"My letter."

"Mm-hmm." Enjoying himself, he slid his hands into his pockets and leaned one shoulder against the doorjamb. His right foot inched unobtrusively over the threshold in a move any door-to-door salesman would envy.

Her eyes widened. "And just because you saw my letter—"

"I decided to drive up and see you."

"Drive up and see me." She nodded, then shook her head. "Just like that?"

"Just like that." The top of her head barely reached his shoulder. He let his gaze wander down to her legs. Not spectacular, but nice. He looked back at her face and cocked an expectant brow. "So, can I come in?"

'Oh. Well . . ." Nibbling on her lush lower lip, she aimed a doubtful look back into the house. "You caught me at a bad—"

"I won't keep you long." What was she, a vestal virgin guarding the temple gates against a horde of pillaging infidels? "I just want to talk to you. Unless . . . Will your husband mind?"

"There is no husband. I'm not—"

"Well, then." Straightening, he stepped smoothly into her personal space, grinning when she backed up.

She heaved a sigh that could have expressed anything from impatience to resignation. Connoisseur that he was, Brent noticed the interesting things a sigh did to the pert breasts under her ratty T-shirt. "Okay, come on in."

The sulky invitation had him swallowing a chuckle. "Thanks. I think I will."

See, that was the thing about dares; they almost always had unpleasant consequences. This particular unpleasant consequence stood between Trash and To Save or Not to Save, big and golden and sexy as sin, smiling temptation's own smile.

It ought to be illegal for a man to look that good in plain old jeans. His shirt was silk, a pale blue that deepened the color of his eyes.

Jen didn't know whether to blame panic, a guilty conscience, or his proximity, but whatever the cause, her heart was racing, she felt light-headed, and she tingled in a way that wasn't altogether pleasant.

If this was sexual chemistry, she didn't like it one bit.

Her eyes had started a side trip down a couple of yards of muscular leg when she realized she was staring. The blush shot into her cheeks, a reaction she'd always resented because it made her so easy to read. She forced her guilty gaze back to his face and noticed he was doing some staring of his own.

That's when Jen remembered the way she was dressed. What her hair looked like. The makeup she hadn't used.

Screaming would be redundant, she thought with an internal sigh. Oh well, at least things couldn't get any worse.

Right on cue, her empty stomach snarled like a wounded jackal. Brent grinned, and it was all she could do not to toss him out on his gorgeous butt. She lifted her chin and gestured toward the stuff piled at his feet. "I was cleaning the closets. I missed lunch."

He gave her a slow insolent once-over that had her fighting the urge to squirm. "It's a good thing."

A good thing? What kind of crack was that? Granted, she was twelve years older than the last time he'd seen her, but if he was implying that she needed to lose weight . . . She scowled at him. "Why?"

"Well, if you hadn't missed lunch, you wouldn't be hungry right now."

All bod and no brains, she decided, but forbore comment.

"And if you weren't hungry right now, I wouldn't be able to take you out to dinner." He flashed his lethal grin. "Would I?"

"Dinner?" She gaped at him. Looked down at her

bag-lady outfit, then back at him. "Now? I don't know—"

"Unless you have plans? I wouldn't want to cause problems with the man in your life."

"There is no man," she muttered absently, still wrestling with confusion.

"Then there's no problem, is there?"

She was starting to say "Well, I guess not" when sanity thundered back. Jennifer Casey go out with Brent Maddox, millionaire playboy? He had to be kidding! Not wanting to appear ungrateful—or as intimidated as she was—she stretched her lips into an imitation regretful smile. "Thanks anyway, Brent, but—"

"I really think you owe it to me, Jen. Under the circumstances."

Off balance again. "Owe it to you?"

"Yep. That letter of yours . . ." His voice faded into silent reproach. She winced. Lord only knew, if that darned letter had caused him a fraction of the grief it had her . . .

The phone rang. *Saved by the bell!* "Excuse me," she murmured, and stepped around him. There was no time for a hello, the caller was already mid-tirade. Mary Jane Williams, *née* Sanders, was *not* pleased by her newfound notoriety.

"But, Mary Jane, I didn't know they would actually—" Jen flinched as the harangue on the other end picked up volume. She turned her back to Brent, held the phone away from her ear, and waited for her opening.

Eventually, even Mary Jane had to pause to breathe. Jen tried again. "I really am sorry. They weren't supposed to print it." The next indignant shriek had her wincing. "They were supposed to forward it." She shot a hunted look over her shoulder. "To Brent."

That little tidbit provoked a squeal of dismay that set Jen's teeth on edge. "I know you're a happily married woman now, Mary Jane. Of course, you didn't really walk into walls. It was a figure of—"

The connection broke with a crack, and Jen grimaced. "I'm sorry." Shoulders slumped, she hung up the phone and turned to face the music. Smiling weakly into Brent's scowl, she explained, "That was Mary Jane."

"Ummm." A muscle flexed in his jaw.

"She's kind of upset about the letter too."

"Is that right?"

"Yes." Jen sighed. "I really am sorry, Brent. It was just a—" Inspiration struck, and she brightened. "I know! I'll send them a retraction!"

"No. No, you won't."

"Why not?"

"Look, Jen. Ever since I did that stupid interview with *Celebrity*, I haven't had a minute's peace. The phone rings off the hook with requests for more interviews. People stop me on the street. My life has turned into one big circus. I haven't even had time to take a—" He broke off and drew what she imagined was a calming breath. "Just when the interview ruckus started to die down, you wrote that letter."

"Oh."

"Oh. Tell me, Jen, did you see Leno last Friday?"

Oh, God. "No."

"Well, suffice it to say, thanks to your letter, my love life is providing raw material for every stand-up comic in the business. I'm hotter than Madonna's underwear these days."

"I'm so sorry," she whispered miserably.

"So you admit you've caused me a lot of grief?" He waited for her penitent nod. "All right, then. I'll pick you up in an hour."

"An hour?" One of them was missing the point. She had a bad feeling it was her. "But—"

"Wear something dressy, okay?" Her stomach gurgled again, and he grinned. "You can get a bite of something to tide you over."

She rubbed her temple, but the conversation didn't get any clearer. "Tide me over?"

"Trust me." He touched the end of her nose. The little jolt that streaked down to her toes forcefully reminded her that she couldn't go anywhere with this man.

"I can't—"

"Sure you can. See you later, Jen." Leaning down, he lightly brushed his lips across hers. It was the kind of meaningless buss a man like him probably gave hundreds of women a day. Unfortunately, Jen wasn't hundreds of women.

Every single nerve ending in her body went on overload. It was the only explanation. Her nerve endings overloaded and her brain synapses shorted out.

Otherwise, she would have chased after him and stopped him before he got out the door. She would have put her foot down in no uncertain terms. Told him she was absolutely *not* going to dinner with him. Not tonight, not ever.

If she'd had a working brain cell left in her head, she never would have drifted, trancelike, into the bathroom. She never would have taken that shower, washed and blow-dried her hair, put on makeup and her best dress, or misted herself with Tendre Poison.

And she certainly wouldn't have been ready and waiting to go forty-five minutes later.

TWO

So far, so good. Maybe she wouldn't have to hunt down Candy and strangle her with her bare hands. Maybe she'd panicked for nothing. Maybe, Jen thought as she relaxed marginally, she should sit back and enjoy her one and only date with an international playboy. "So where are you taking me?"

"It's a surprise."

"Uh-huh. This surprise destination wouldn't involve cement galoshes and a large body of water, would it?"

He looked thoughtful. "Now *there's* an idea."

"Forget I said anything." She paused. "I really am sorry."

"So you said. You know, I didn't remember you at first."

Jen smiled wryly. "I didn't think you would."

"It all came back to me after I pulled out the yearbook: Jennifer Marie Casey, straight-A student and president of the Poetry Club." He shot her a glance then looked back to the broad, tree-lined streets of

San Luis Obispo. "I never would've pegged you for a poison-pen artist."

Just the slightest bit miffed at being "pegged" as both forgettable *and* a wimp, Jen said, "Well, we all have our little talents."

"Yeah, but you always seemed like such a nice girl."

Make that a forgettable, *dull* wimp. But what could she say? "I am."

"So why'd you write that letter?"

Turning her head, she eyed him judiciously. "I think I will take the Fifth on that one."

"Aha! Secrets." He grinned. "I'll worm it out of you sooner or later."

He was probably a champion wormer-outer, especially if his victim was a woman. Good thing he wouldn't have time to work his wiles on her. She faced forward. "My lips are sealed."

Slanting him a covert glance a few seconds later, she wondered where he'd come up with the suit. Brent Maddox in a gray suit—Italian and silk, probably—white shirt, and striped tie was a sight to bring more sophisticated women than her to their knees. Of course he packed a pretty hefty punch in faded jeans too.

Suddenly it was all she could do not to drop her head back against the Jaguar's plush leather seat and groan out loud. Why did her quietly simmering hormones have to start perking over this man? Given Brent's well-publicized taste in women, her awakening hormones were wasting their time; they weren't going to have a chance to actually *do* anything.

Not that she wanted them to, of course.

So why didn't they just simmer down?

All at once Jen pictured herself as a pot of furiously bubbling liquid that, left unattended, boiled itself right out of existence. This was not a pretty picture. Maybe she should grab Bernie and run for the nearest drive-in.

"The old hometown hasn't changed much, has it?"

"Not much."

"I gather Mary Jane is married?"

Jen grimaced. "Well, she was married as of this evening. I can't vouch for her marital status if Biff sees that letter."

"Biff Williams?"

"One and the same. He still doesn't like you, by the way. As a matter of fact, he's been known to snarl at the mere mention of your name."

Brent looked ridiculously pleased. "Is that right? Hell, I only took Mary Jane out to the lake once. How was I supposed to know those two were going together?"

"Hmm."

"So what's old Biff doing these days?"

"He's a life insurance salesman," she said, and laughed along with Brent.

Twelve years ago Biff Williams had spent most of his time threatening to help people *out* of life. His favorite opening gambit consisted of a shove, a growl, and, "Hey, twerp, is your insurance paid up?"

"God, I love irony." Brent shook his head. "What about Marci DiBoccatella?"

Another old girlfriend. Jen subdued a malicious grin. This one would knock him for a loop. "She's a nun."

"You're kidding!" Brent turned to gape. "A nun? Marci DiBoccatella is a *nun?*"

The grin broke free. "Yep. For eight years, up in San Francisco. Her name's Sister Mary Serenity now."

"I don't believe it. Marci DiBoccatella, a nun. My God, she had the biggest—"

"*Yes?*"

"—smile," he finished smoothly. "Marci had a very impressive smile."

"Right." Jen snorted, and tried not to think about the fact that her "smile" was a third as impressive as Marci's.

Stop it! Stop comparing yourself to the other women he's gone out with, or you'll make a fool of yourself when you hide under the car seat. Geez, the pitfalls a woman dropped into when she dated a dreamboat! Keeping up with the Daphnes and Marcis of the world was murder on the self-esteem.

Thank goodness she only had this one dinner to get through. Things could be worse.

Then they arrived at Brent's surprise destination. Things got worse.

"Henri's?" Even Donnertonians knew about this place. Very posh. Very chic. Very, very expensive. Jen's hard-won ease evaporated.

"Yep. Best French cuisine this side of the Left Bank." Brent tossed a theatrical kiss off his fingertips.

He should know, she mused nervously, watching him stroll around to open her door. He'd been to the Left Bank—and everywhere else—she remembered with growing trepidation. Aside from a four-year stint at Sac State, she'd never been out of Donnerton. What was she doing here?

Oblivious to her mounting anxiety, Brent helped her out of the car. "I haven't been here in months. When I decided to come see you, I tossed a suit in the car and called for reservations. We're lucky they could work us in."

"Lucky." Right. Like passengers on the *Titanic* were lucky.

Henri's delivered everything its reputation promised. Multileveled, dotted with lush greenery, the dining room was bordered by an immaculate bank of windows. Mozart wafted unobtrusively through the muted clink of fine silver against bone china and the murmur of conversation.

The maître d', a tall and tuxedo-clad man with a mane of silver hair, looked down his long Gallic nose at the fashionable man and woman standing in front of Jen. With a disdainful twitch of his neat mustache, he informed them that no one was seated *sans réservation*. Properly intimidated, ruthlessly dismissed, the Henri's wannabes slunked out the door.

Jen's palms grew damp. "Oh, Lord."

Brent chuckled. "Close. That's Henri."

"He's terrifying."

"Nah, Henri's a pussycat. You'll see."

When the great Henri caught sight of Brent, the transformation from lofty contempt to dignified obsequiousness was nothing short of amazing. But then Brent had a reservation.

"*Bonsoir*, Monsieur Maddox. It's good to see you again. I have your usual table, of course."

Brent slid her a what-did-I-tell-you? glance. "It's good to be back, Henri," he greeted, and Jen almost jumped out of her sedate white pumps when Brent tucked a hand at the small of her back to urge her after the maître d'.

Once they were seated, an imperious snap of Henri's fingers conjured up an equally imposing waiter. Brent ordered wine, served after a ceremonious sniff and taste, and they were left to peruse their menus.

Jen's attention wandered between her menu and her fellow diners. She smoothed a hand over the lace collar of her tea-length blue crepe, feeling like a little brown hen trapped in a flock of peacocks. Brent, on the other hand, fit right in. The gorgeous rat.

"You look fine."

"Thanks, I—" She broke off to frown at him. "How did you know what I was thinking?"

"Sweetheart, I can read you like a book."

"Hmmph." Steadfastly ignoring the way his drawled *sweetheart* tripped her pulse, Jen looked back at the menu. Of course he could read her like a book. He could probably read any woman like a book. The darned man had his own personal library of them.

Ponderous minutes ticked by before she wiggled in discomfort, and Brent said, "What's wrong?"

"They're staring at us," she told her menu.

"Who?"

"Everybody."

Brent glanced around then shook his head. "Nobody's staring at us. Will you relax?"

They were too staring. She could feel their eyes on her—like ants crawling all over her body. Not that she blamed them. They were probably wondering what a woman like her was doing in a place like this with a man like Brent. She was wondering the same thing herself.

Why hadn't she stayed home?

Knock it off! she scolded herself. *What kind of wimp are you, anyway? What do you care what they think? You'll never see these people again.* Heck, she didn't *want* to see them again.

"Anything look good to you?"

Pay attention, Jennifer! "Well, let me see. . . ."

Everything looked good, but then French was a very attractive language. She spoke just enough of it to steer clear of any dish featuring the word *escargot*. Other than that, she was completely in *le dark*. Still, pride demanded she at least try to choose her own dinner.

Ris de veau au gratin caught her eye. Okay. *Au gratin* meant cheese. Probably. *Ris* might be rice. It sounded promising, but pride aside, it never hurt to hedge your bets. She pointed. "What's this?"

Brent leaned in to peer over the edge of her menu. Light slid through the gilded waves of his hair. The spicy musk of his cologne wafted toward her, and she had an irrational urge to take a long, appreciative sniff.

"Sweetbreads *au gratin*."

That certainly quashed the urge. Obviously, *escargot* wasn't the only word one needed to avoid in French restaurants. She tried again. "How about this?"

"Cervelles en matelote?"

"Yes." The way it rolled off his tongue was almost musical. Anything that sounded *that* good couldn't possibly—

"Calf's brains in red wine with mushrooms and onions."

—live up to its name. He chuckled, and she realized her moue of distaste hadn't been entirely mental. She grinned good-naturedly. "Guess my secret's out—I'm no gourmet. I'm almost afraid to ask you to translate anything else."

"How about if I order for us both?"

Jen deliberated. "Okay, but I'd consider it a personal favor if you didn't order garden pests, gray matter, or reproductive organs. And feet," she added hastily when he signaled the waiter. "Let's definitely stay away from feet."

"So after Dad retired from the quarry, he and Mom moved to Sun City. Retirement agrees with them." Across the table Jen grinned. "According to Mom's latest letter, their love life is the hottest thing in Arizona these days." Then she blushed.

Brent stifled his own grin in favor of a dramatic sigh. "Meanwhile, their lovely young daughter molders away in the backwater time forgot, ignorant of the exciting possibilities waiting just outside the city limits. What made you decide to bury yourself in Donnerton, anyway?"

She shrugged. "It seemed like the thing to do at the time. And I'm not moldering." She paused thoughtfully. "At least, not much. Not all of us can be adventurous, *bon vivant* jet-setters, you know."

"Is that what I am?"

"Among other things." He was about to pin her down on those "other things" when she added, "I've seen my share of the world, it was just smaller than yours."

"How small?"

"Sacramento."

"Ah."

"I'll let you get away with that condescending response because according to the article in *Celebrity*, you've been just about everywhere. You've earned your right to condescend."

"Thanks." Brent hid a wince at the mention of that damned article.

He hadn't given much thought to his lifestyle until he'd seen it bared like a centerfold, but there had been a bad taste in his mouth ever since. Set down in black and white, and in a four-page spread with full-color pictures, his life seemed selfish and meaningless. He'd been fighting the image of himself as a thirty-two-year-old social butterfly for weeks.

"Did your parents travel with you?"

"My mother did. Dad died of a heart attack right after I graduated from college."

Jen's brown eyes went liquid with sympathy. "Oh, Brent, I'm so sorry. I didn't know. As I remember, they were very close. Your mother must have taken it hard."

"She did." Then he told her what he'd never told anyone. "I came close to losing her, too. That's how all the traveling started, as a matter of fact. Keeping her busy and on the move was the only thing that seemed to help. So we traveled: London, Paris, the Riviera. We even went on a safari." And somewhere along the way, "therapy" became habit.

"But she's all right now?"

He grinned. "Better than all right. She's getting married again."

"Does she have your blessing?"

"Sure. Mom's the marrying kind and Jack Hansen will treat her right."

Jen's eyes narrowed shrewdly. "Let me guess. Your mom's the marrying kind, but you aren't."

"Good guess. I'm not getting married for a long time." If ever. "How about you?"

She smiled ruefully. "Oh, I'm the marrying kind, all right. Mine are your typical middle-class dreams."

"Hearth and home?"

She nodded. "And don't forget career. This is the liberated version of the middle-class dream."

"That's right, you teach. I guess you like it, huh?"

"I love it." Her tone was dry, but her eyes glowed with fierce enthusiasm. "Teaching English lit. to teenagers borders on masochism, but I have to admit there's nothing quite as satisfying as leading adolescents to the waters of Keats and Shakespeare. Even if I can't make them drink."

The waiter arrived with their entrées. Brent leaned back in his chair and tried to remember the last time he felt that enthusiastic about anything. Not for years, he realized suddenly.

Irritated by the unwelcome insight, he scowled. He had more money than China had tea. Nine out of ten Americans would kill to be in his shoes. And he was bored stiff, and had been for some time.

He shifted restlessly, trying to brush the whole idea off as stupid. But the train of thought hurtled on in spite of his best effort.

Was he playing at life? What real reason did he have to get up in the morning?

Before Cousin Graham's windfall changed everything, Brent had wanted to be an architect. Knowing he would need a scholarship, he'd been prepared to work hard. It wasn't one of the things most people tended to remember about him, but all through high school he'd been among the top ten percent of his class.

Thanks to Cousin Graham's twenty-five mil, he hadn't had to worry about scholarships. Oh, he'd gone to Princeton—he even had the degree to prove it—but the only subject he'd excelled in was Party Hearty 101. He'd more or less blown off a top-notch education.

More shaken than he wanted to admit and bristling with resentment because of it, he glared across the table. Damn woman was messing with his peace of mind. Dredging up a bunch of bourgeois values he thought he'd ditched for good.

But his annoyance melted when he noticed Jen frowning suspiciously as she pushed her food around her plate. He shook his head.

Cute. From her shoulder-length pageboy to her doe eyes and button nose, Jen Casey had it in spades. Even her clothes were cute. The only noncute thing about her was her mouth. Everything else was *Rebecca of Sunnybrook Farm*; her mouth was *Frederick's of Hollywood*.

She leaned in to sniff at her plate, and he told himself to stop fantasizing about her mouth and put her out of her misery. "Don't you trust me, Jen?"

She gave him a quizzical glance. "Trust you?"

"Look, I know you're hungry. You should be eating your dinner, not playing with it. So I've got to figure you're thinking garden pests here."

"I'm always cautious around food I can't pronounce," she mumbled.

Giving her an understanding nod, he asked, "Can you say 'veal scallops'?"

Her wide-eyed look of relief was almost comical. "Veal! Why didn't you tell me?" she said, and dug in.

Brent grinned and shook his head. "Damned if I'm not starting to like you, Jennifer Casey."

She swallowed daintily. "And that surprises you? I'm generally considered a very likable person."

"You *did* write that letter."

She squirmed, looking guilty. "Well, yes, but I did say I was—"

"You screamed and slammed the door in my face too."

A blush painted her cheekbones. "That was rude, but you caught me at a bad—"

"I had to guilt-trip you into having dinner with me."

She huffed. "Okay, I'm a shrew. So why are you starting to like me?"

He shrugged. "I just am, that's all."

"Well, aside from your annoying habit of bullying your way into places where you're not wanted, and your deplorable talent for emotional blackmail, you're not so bad yourself."

"I'll try not let all that faint praise go to my head. Now eat."

He picked up his fork, wondering what she'd think if he admitted to finding her refreshing.

It had been years since he'd been around anybody whose reactions were as unguarded as Jen's. Most of the people he ran with these days were either too jaded to have reactions, or too sophisticated to let them show. Jen's thoughts might as well flash across her forehead in red neon. All he needed was a camera.

Shot number one would have been Jen, dazed and fascinated and looking him over when he finally managed to get into her house. It would be followed by a picture of her fiery blush when she realized she'd been looking him over appraisingly. Then he'd capture her horrified dismay when she remembered that god-awful getup she'd been wearing.

There were other shots he'd like to have: The way she'd wrinkled up her nose at the thought of eating calf's brains. The endearing, self-conscious glances she kept sneaking around the restaurant that made him want to wrap her in his arms and murmur, "It's all right, baby. I won't let them hurt you."

But the snapshot he'd most like to have would be one of her face right after he'd kissed her. There wasn't a man alive who wouldn't get big-headed knowing he could make a woman stupid with a kiss he'd give a maiden aunt.

It left him wondering what Jen would do if he gave her a real kiss. And battling the almost irresistible urge to find out.

Fate seemed to lend a hand when, over *baba au rhum*, Jen said, "Not that I knew you that well in high school, but I would have expected you to change more."

Brent leaned forward, resting one arm on the table. "You think I haven't changed?"

She shrugged. "Well, of course you've changed in some ways. You're more sophisticated, for one thing."

Sophisticated was good. "Yeah?"

"Mm-hmm." She spooned up cake and rum syrup, adding absently, "But basically you're the same cheerful, cocky guy I remember."

Brent frowned. "Cocky?"

She smiled. "Cocky in the nicest possible way, of course."

"Of course." He drummed his fingers on the tablecloth. "And you expected maybe, something else?"

"To tell you the truth, I expected you to be patronizing. Pretentious in a *nouveau riche* kind of way." She tossed it off with light humor, but he didn't believe she was kidding. Not for a minute.

His jaw tightened ominously. "Let me get this straight. You thought the money would turn me into some pretentious jerk?"

It seemed to occur to her, belatedly, that she might be insulting him. Her cheeks pinkened. "I really didn't mean—"

"Would coming into money make *you* pretentious?"

"Oh, I'm not the rich and famous type," she babbled nervously. "That whole lifestyle always seemed kind of pointless to me."

"Pointless?" Her words struck a newly tender spot.

The look on his face must have been something, because Jen's eyes widened as she stumbled into an explanation. "Not pointless, exactly. Just sort of narcissistic. I . . . I mean, well, money *is* the root of all evil. . . . Well, not all evil, but . . ."

He tuned her out while he struggled with the urge to tell her exactly what he thought of twenty-eight-year-old virgin (he was sure of it) high-school teachers who didn't know squat about the real world.

When the epiphany came, it was almost blinding.

He'd been a lot of things since Jen Casey stuck her nose into his life—amused, confused, and mad as hell. Bored he hadn't been. The creeping boredom he hadn't even noticed until recently was gone!

For now. But what would happen when she wasn't around anymore? Would he sink back into the doldrums? He didn't want to chance it. That meant he'd just have to keep her around for a while, at least until he figured out what she had that he'd been missing.

But how? He knew enough about women to know Jen's reluctance to go out with him had been genuine. Reluctance, hell. The woman flat out hadn't wanted anything to do with him. Once she got home, she wouldn't want anything to do with him again. So how was he going to get her to hang around?

Just then he heard her say, ". . . can't imagine what somebody with that kind of money would do all day."

And Brent replied, "I think you should find out for yourself."

Her spoon halted in midair. She stared. "Excuse me?"

"I said I think you should find out for yourself what rich people do all day."

"Find out for myself?" He nodded. "You're kidding."

"Nope."

She snorted. "And how do you suggest I do that? Watch a couple hundred *Lifestyles of the Rich and Famous* reruns?"

"Uh-uh. Come back to L.A. with me for a few days. A week," he amended hastily. No sense taking chances, a week would give him plenty of time to figure this out. "For seven days, you can go where I go and do what I do. Get your information firsthand."

"I don't think so."

Time for a shot to that middle-class pride. He nodded. "No guts, huh?"

That sparked the light of battle. "That's not true."

"So what's the problem?"

She shook her head slowly, but the glint in her eyes told him she was intrigued. "Well, the problem is you're crazy."

Brent dropped his voice into the low-seductive-murmur range, well aware of what it did to a woman's common sense. "Come on, Jen. What's so crazy about a week of fun in the sun? Give it a try. I dare you."

"Darn it, Brent, I really wish you hadn't said that."

The ride home from Henri's was a silent one, mostly because Jen was racking her brain to find a way out. Brent knew it, of course, so when she hesitated outside her door, ready to spring the old lunch-date-with-Candy excuse, he smirked. "Welshing, Jen?"

Her chin shot up. "I'll be packed in twenty minutes."

Brent didn't know it, but he almost lost her when the car rounded the last curve in his mile-long driveway and she got her first eyeful of his home. Perched on a steep hill overlooking a pristine beach, the sprawling hacienda with its red tile roof was beautiful, intimidatingly beautiful. God only knew how far and fast she would have run if she wasn't strapped to a Jaguar just then.

As it was, there was no escaping the spacious rooms with their high ceilings and limestone floors.

The furniture tended toward low, sleek, and leather, leaving color to scattered hand-woven rugs and dramatic artwork.

The bedroom he picked out for her was different. "This is Mom's room when she visits," he explained, and shrugged self-consciously. "She likes antiques."

You had to hand it to the man, though, he was smooth.

"It's beautiful, Brent."

"I'm glad you like it." He smiled. "Just let me know if you need anything," he said. "See you in the morning," he said, stepped up, and kissed her.

But unlike the light brush he'd given her before, this kiss meant business.

The earth tilted at least ninety degrees, forcing Jen to gasp, clutch at his shoulders, and hang on for dear life when she should have pulled away. Within seconds, pulling away ceased to be an option.

His mouth was warm and firm and he knew just what to do with it. God, he tasted good. He angled his head, his tongue gliding along the seam in her lips, and her breath tangled in her lungs while her heart thundered in her ears. Opening her mouth wasn't an option—it was absolute necessity. A growl rumbled up from his chest, and the kiss exploded.

His tongue rimmed her parted lips, before sliding into her mouth. The penetration—slow, slick, and potent—had her moaning and plastering herself against that long, hard body from breast to thigh. Rising on tiptoe, she rubbed against him, opening her mouth wider.

Her last coherent thought was that whoever said a kiss was just a kiss had never kissed Brent Maddox.

A split second before she went crazy and started

tearing off his shirt, he lifted his head. She thought, *Why did we stop?* right before she remembered that they shouldn't have started in the first place.

She wondered if she looked half as stunned as he did during the subsequent heavy breathing and staring. Finally, he dropped the strong arms that had somehow gotten wrapped around her. Taking a step back, shaking his head, he muttered something that sounded like, "Big mistake," before walking away, leaving her to grind her teeth through a restless night filled with incredibly erotic dreams.

THREE

Somebody was playing the "Anvil Chorus" on her skull with the unpleasant end of a claw hammer. The ache pulsed through the heavy shroud of sleep, tugging Jen toward unwelcome consciousness. Even in her near-comatose state, she could taste the Mojave Desert, half of which seemed to be piled in her mouth. An unearthly creak ground in her ears.

It penetrated gradually—the unearthly creak came from her molars. Still three-quarters asleep, she managed to relax her jaws, then winced and swallowed miserably. Her eyes opened to gritty slits, and a hazy room swam into view.

But it wasn't her room.

Cautiously—because if she moved it, her throbbing head would topple off her shoulders—she slid her eyeballs left. Definitely not her room. She didn't own an antique cherrywood armoire that looked to be in mint condition. Or that beautiful matching dresser complete with porcelain pitcher and bowl.

Maybe she was still dreaming.

She lifted a hand toward her pounding head, hoping the press of fingers would stop the percussion session so she could think. Delicate white lace fluttered at her wrist. She squinted—a terrible mistake. The vise squeezing her brains clamped down mercilessly, wringing out a moan. Complete stillness suddenly seemed like a good idea.

She dropped her arm, closed her eyes, and waited. When the pain subsided to a bearable level, she dragged up her heavy eyelids and raised her arm again.

It was a lovely nightgown, she mused groggily. White, long-sleeved, sort of . . . Victorian. Obviously expensive.

But whose was it?

Her bewildered gaze drifted up to the magnificent silk canopy that capped the four-poster bed. She tried to remember where she'd seen one like it.

Oh, yes. That picture of the English manor house that had belonged to one of Queen Victoria's ladies-in-waiting. Jen's sluggish brain grappled with the question of how she'd come to be lying in a one-hundred-fifty-year-old bed that looked brand-new.

Time travel. It whispered through the fog in her head, and she frowned blearily. Time travel? Didn't that only happen in romance novels? Her groggy gaze straggled around the elegant, unfamiliar room. Evidently not.

But how? And why? Her forehead wrinkled thoughtfully, spearing a nasty pain from temple to temple. She groaned again. God, what if they hadn't invented aspirin yet?

She was still struggling toward clear thinking when the ring of a telephone ripped away the last sleepy cobwebs. The instrument on the bedside table warbled again, then fell silent as somebody, somewhere picked up.

Jen now faced an entirely new set of problems. She'd seen roadkill that had to have felt better than she did at the moment. Feeling like a total moron on top of that was a bonus she could have easily done without. *Time travel.* She must have slipped a cog.

Remembering where she was and how she'd gotten there convinced her of it.

She was in Brent Maddox's Malibu hideaway by the sea, and she'd landed herself here by swallowing his dare like a bait-hungry trout. Sighing morosely, she wondered aloud, "When am I going to learn?"

Not soon enough to save her from this latest, and direst, consequence.

"He's going to be a problem," she mumbled. "A big, sexy problem." Just thinking about it gave a new twist to her tension headache, and sent her grumbling into the bathroom.

She barely spared a glance for the luxurious peach-and-cream marble bath before her gaze snagged on the wild woman in the mirror. Her hair looked like somebody had combed it with an eggbeater, her eyes were puffy and bloodshot. All in all, it was a pretty scary sight. But then even at her best, she wasn't the kind of woman who would attract Brent Maddox.

If only the reverse were true.

Jen scowled at the Jen scowling back at her. "So you're attracted to him. Big deal. Any woman with an ounce of blood in her veins would be attracted to him. It just proves you're healthy. But you listen to me, sister, *no more kissing!* We're nipping this thing in the bud, right now!"

God only knew why he'd kissed her in the first place, but odds were he wouldn't do it again. Just the same, she'd keep a three-yard safety zone between them from here on out. Any man who could turn your brain into a puddle of useless gray goo with one kiss was more than dangerous—he was lethal. Repeated contact with that mouth, and brain damage could prove irreversible.

"Just keep your distance," she reminded her reflection, tugging Mrs. Maddox's nightgown off over her head. She'd been too flustered last night to remember to pack her own. "Think cool, calm, and in control. You can keep your hands off him for a week." She could.

It took forty-five minutes, another pep talk with aspirin, a shower, makeup, and her blow-dryer, but Jen finally rejoined the human race. Her white linen pants and jade polo looked crisp, nondescript, and unprovocative. She'd just strapped on her white sandals when somebody knocked.

She knew exactly who it was. Given that and the effect the knowledge had on her heart rate, *Come in* didn't seem like an especially intelligent response. But what could she say? "Come in."

The door swung open, and Brent strolled in. *Just like he owns the place*, she thought waspishly. Which, of course, he did. When she realized she was grinding her teeth again, she forced herself to stop. Then he smiled, and her stomach did a neat little back flip.

I am in deep . . . swamp sludge, she groaned silently. She looked from Brent's beautiful white teeth up to his watchful blue eyes, and couldn't quite suppress a tiny shiver. *Yep, swamp sludge. And up to my ears in big, hungry alligators.*

"Good morning." Brent crossed the room, her wary gaze tracking him all the way. "You don't have to worry, you know."

Her lips curved wryly. "What makes you think I'm worried?"

"You've got that what-big-teeth-you-have look in your eye. Don't worry, honey, you're safe with me." She mumbled something. "What was that?"

"I said, too bad I'm not safe with myself." She shrugged and gestured to the room. "Anyway, here we are."

"Yeah." And excitement was singing through his veins. Which was damn silly when you thought about it, because he barely knew the woman. "It was the dare, wasn't it?"

Jen crinkled her nose. "You figured that out, huh?"

"Eventually. I have to admit it surprised the hell out of me, though. Who would have thought Jennifer Casey, devotee of the Bard and respected high-school English teacher would be a sucker for a dare?" His eyebrows lifted. "Any dare?"

She nodded glumly. "Evidently."

"Tell me," he said, and sat next to her on the bed.

She talked, he studied. Seen in the bright light of day, Jen was about as sophisticated as a rookie Girl Scout. Nothing about her suggested a kiss that packed the kick of a Missouri mule.

Hell, he'd kissed her in the first place only because

his curiosity got the better of him. He'd wondered about her reaction.

Well, now he knew how the proverbial killed cat felt. Damned if the woman hadn't caught fire in his arms. Which was all well and good, except he'd gotten scorched in the backfire. It had taken a long, acrobatic night tossing on his bed, trying to forget that kiss and convince himself his reaction had been a fluke.

Just then Jen caught his attention by moistening her lips, and his breath shortened. Or maybe not such a fluke.

Forget the mouth, he ordered himself, but it was easier thought than done. Of course that was before Jen helped him out.

"I ironed my hair on a dare," she admitted.

He blinked. "Why in God's name would you do that?"

"To straighten it, of course. All the girls were doing it."

Maybe she hadn't noticed. "Your hair *is* straight."

"You're thinking like a grown man. Teenage girls operate on a different system of logic."

He snorted. "Right. So what happened?"

"Burned away a big, triangular wedge." She pointed to the back of her head. "Right here. I was going to go to the Cut 'N Curl to get it evened out, but Terry Sudman dared me not to."

"She always was a snot."

Jen beamed approvingly. "Yeah. Anyway, she dared me to go to school with it like that, so I did. For three months."

He tried to picture her with an inverted-V hairdo. "Sorry, I missed that."

"Thank God." She paused, then blurted, "I wrote that letter to *Celebrity* on a dare too."

Amusement vanished. His eyebrows snapped together. "You subjected me to public—"

"They weren't supposed to print it. They were supposed to forward it to you."

Brent clenched his jaw tightly.

"It was a triple-dog dare," she offered hopefully, and his sense of humor bounced back.

"Oh, well, that's different." Shaking his head, he said, "Anybody ever tell you that you're your own worst enemy?"

She sighed morosely. "I know." Then, slanting him a look, "So where does that leave us?"

"I don't follow."

"Now that you know about my fatal weakness—"

"Your Achilles' heel, so to speak?"

"Exactly. You're not going to use it against me, are you?"

It wasn't hard to see where she was coming from. Stroking his chin, he pretended to mull it over. "I don't know. . . . The possibilities are endless—and tempting."

"Brent—"

"But I'll pass. That is, as long as you're not planning to renege on last night's dare."

Jen scowled indignantly. "I never renege."

Satisfaction brought a smile to his face. "I didn't think so."

Her gaze dropped to the bedspread, where she traced invisible circles. "The thing is . . . now that you've got me where you want me, I'd like to discuss terms."

"Terms?" he murmured absently. The phrase

you've got me where you want me spawned a string of ideas he had no business getting. She wasn't his type, for God's sake! Or hadn't been, before that kiss.

"You dared me to stay with you for a week, right?"

He dragged his mind out of the gutter and back where it belonged. "Right. So?"

Blushing furiously, she cleared her throat. "So maybe we could define 'stay with.' "

Without thinking, he reached out to brush a soft, rosy cheek. She froze, and he dropped his hand. "Just stay with me and keep me company. We'll get to know each other better. Okay?" Damn, but he wished she wouldn't lick her lips like that.

"But last night . . ."

"Last night I kissed you." Jen nodded. "Should I apologize? I will if you want me to, but I've got to tell you, sweetheart . . . I wouldn't mean it."

Her gaze zoomed up to his face. Judging from her expression, she didn't know whether to thank him or head for the hills. "You wouldn't?" Lips twitching, he shook his head. "Well . . . I'd rather you didn't do it again."

It amazed the hell out of him, but he couldn't bring himself to agree. "I won't do anything you don't want me to do."

Relief raced across her expressive face. Lord, the woman was naive. It evidently hadn't dawned on her that he could make her want, period. "Thanks."

"Reprieved?" Brent gazed toward the ceiling. "The woman is very hard on my ego."

Genuinely distressed, she protested, "Oh, but I didn't mean . . . That is, it's not you. I just don't . . ."

"Fool around? I know." She looked so embarrassed, he had to laugh. "It's nothing to be ashamed of, you know."

"What?"

"Virginity."

Her face went up in flames. "Oh, God."

Finding out he was right about her innocence didn't surprise him, but the spark of interest it kindled did. Brent smothered that spark like Smokey the Bear. Sex was easy to come by; he wanted something else from Jen. He couldn't explain his belief that she was the key to rediscovering the joy in day-to-day living, but he trusted his instincts. She was here, she was staying, and he wasn't bored. It was enough.

For now.

Determined to put her at ease again, he asked, "Aren't you curious about the week's agenda?"

It looked to be muscle by muscle, but she relaxed. "Sure."

"Let's see . . . this afternoon, I thought we'd go down to the club. We can get in a quick set before dinner."

"Tennis? Uh, listen, Brent. This is probably as good a time as any to tell you I'm not the most athletic person to jog down the pike. Candy's tried to whip me into shape." Her hands lifted in defeat. "I'm just unwhippable."

"Who's Candy?"

"Candy Johnson, my best friend. She's the girls' gym teacher at Donnerton, and every month or so she tries to drag me, kicking and screaming, into the ranks of the physically fit. She means well, and she's harmless. Most of the time. There was one nasty incident involving Rollerblades, that— Never mind."

He chuckled. "Don't stop now."

She shook her head. "Trust me, you don't want to hear it—it's not a pretty story. In fact, I get queasy all over again just thinking about it."

"Well, we won't need the EMTs tomorrow. Tennis is a low-risk sport."

"Not the way I play," she said, and her air of gloomy resignation almost made him laugh.

"One day while you're here, I thought we'd go for a sail. Oh, and there's the charity benefit on Friday."

"I've never been sailing. I think I'd like to try it. But I'm afraid I don't have a thing to wear at an upscale charity benefit." She didn't sound too broken up about it.

He stood and reached for her hand, tugging her to her feet. "Which is why we're going shopping this morning," he declared as he towed her toward the door.

Jen gaped as if he'd just announced an invasion of little green men. "I can't afford the kind of dress you wear to a function like that."

"I can."

Her no-kidding snort segued into a mulish pout. "You are not buying me clothes."

Actually, he kind of liked the idea. What would she look like in something with a little pizzazz? He decided then and there to find out. All he had to do was convince Jen.

At the top of the wide staircase he stopped, pulling her around to face him. He hit her with his best cajoling smile. "Come on, Jen, let me buy you the dress."

"No."

In a move that never failed to get him what he

wanted from a woman, he trailed an index finger down her throat, resting his fingertip over the pulse that took off rabbit quick. He looked into her eyes and murmured, "Please?"

Her breath caught. She shivered delicately and crumbled like an oatmeal cookie. "Okay."

"Thanks, honey." Then, before she could voice the objection already dawning in her eyes: "Come on, we'd better get down to breakfast. Crampton doesn't like to be kept waiting."

She looked so confused, he almost kissed her again. "Crampton?"

They started down the stairs. "Althea Crampton, my housekeeper. You didn't meet her last night, because we got in too late, but there's no escaping her this morning. Don't worry, I'll protect you."

Jen chuckled nervously. "You make her sound worse than the Spanish Inquisition."

"Just wait."

The hacienda's breakfast nook was tucked in a sunny alcove where a row of wide windows framed the blue Pacific. Jen caught just a brief glimpse of sparkling sea and sand before her gaze hooked on the woman standing next to the round glass table.

Althea Crampton looked like a cross between a lady wrestler and Brünnhilde, only meaner. She had the alert, beady black eyes of a hawk, and the beaklike nose to match. Every iron-gray hair on her head marched tidily up into the bun perched on her crown. Not one wrinkle marred her short-sleeved black dress, giving one the distinct impression that the material had been starched then ruthlessly ironed into submission.

Brent's housekeeper had a stare a hanging judge would envy. It nailed Jen before shifting to Brent. "Been at it again, I see."

He pulled out a chair, and Jen sank into it, amazed to see color wash his cheekbones. "I have not. This is an old high-school friend of mine. She's spending the week."

Althea's shrewd gaze swung back to Jen, raking in every detail. She looked skeptical. "Old high-school friend, are you?" Jen nodded. "You got a name?"

"Jen. Jennifer Casey." The *ma'am* was understood.

Eyes narrowed, Althea crossed her arms over her chest. Tense seconds ticked by. Then: "The letter."

Uh-oh. Brent met Jen's mute appeal with a grin and a shrug. She forced herself to meet Crampton's obsidian stare. "Yes, I wrote the letter. But I—"

"Good work." The housekeeper gave a curt nod. "Eat your breakfast." It was an order, given as she marched away.

Brent's jaw dropped. "Good work? *Good work?* Just whose side is she on, anyway?" He glared at Althea's departing back. "You know, for two cents I'd fire that woman. The only thing is . . ."

"Yes?"

He reached for his orange juice and muttered, "She wouldn't go." Jen fought a chuckle, and lost. "You think that's funny, huh?"

"Sure. Here you are, a sophisticated man of the world, adored and sought after by women everywhere, and henpecked by your own housekeeper." A fact Jen found both surprising and endearing. Maybe there was more guy-next-door left in the suave play-boy than she'd thought. She picked up her spoon. "I take it she's been with you for a while?"

"Five years. Mom took the old housekeeper with her when she moved into her own place and hired Crampton to take care of things around here. I'm not sure, but I think there was a bloodless coup within the first twenty-four hours. I lost."

"Tough customer, huh?"

"You don't know the half of it."

"She does seem sort of . . . brusque," Jen finished diplomatically.

Brent cocked his head. "She *was* brusque with you, wasn't she?" He nodded. "Well, congratulations."

"For?"

"You made Crampton's A-list. Brusque is reserved for people she likes. Everybody else gets downright rude. She's got Daphne Carlson afraid to set foot through the front door."

Good for you, Althea, Jen decided, and ran her tongue over her teeth. "Cramps your style, does she?"

"She gives it her best shot."

Jen gestured to the two bowls of fresh fruit, basket of flaky croissants, and steaming pot of coffee arranged on the table. "At least she takes good care of you."

"Yeah." Brent scooped a plump strawberry out of his bowl. "Some days she even lets me be the boss."

FOUR

Death by strangulation was too good for Candy John-
son. Too merciful. Too quick. Jen glowered out the
Jag's window and contemplated the virtues of torture
Apache-style.

Brent was taking her shopping on Rodeo Drive.
Rodeo Drive, for crying out loud! The last rodeo she'd
gone to had had the words *Twenty-fifth Annual Wild
West* tacked in front of its name.

One way or the other, Candy was dead meat.

"You're awfully quiet. Is something wrong?"

Jen rolled her eyes heavenward. "Didn't I *tell* him
I didn't want to shop in these stores? Didn't I *beg* him
to take me someplace sensible, like Penney's? Is he
completely *ignoring* my every word?" Facing Brent,
she smiled sweetly. "Whatever gave you the ridiculous idea that something is wrong?"

"Oh, I don't know," he drawled. "The pout,
maybe? The cold shoulder I've been getting for the
last half hour? You did say I could buy you a dress,"
he reminded her.

"I also said I didn't want you to buy me an *expensive* dress."

Brent angled the Jag into a parking space. "Expensive is relative, and I don't see what difference it makes. If I don't mind spending my money, why should you?"

Flabbergasted, she could only stare. "Is that your usual approach? Have wallet, will travel? No wonder your love life is in such a mess!"

"My love life," he growled, reaching for the door handle, "is just fine, thank you."

"That's a matter of opinion."

"And I don't remember asking for yours." He slid out of the car.

Jen's brow furrowed. Didn't he realize his cavalier, come-spend-with-me attitude only encouraged the kind of gold digger he'd complained about in *Celebrity?* Evidently not. Good Lord, somebody had to set him straight.

As the only somebody available, Jen pounced the minute he opened her door. "Do the women you date usually expect—"

"We are not here to talk about my love life. We are here to buy you a dress."

Jen crossed her arms. "I'd rather talk about your love life."

Bracing one hand atop the car, he leaned in, giving her the kind of smile best left behind bedroom doors. "I had no idea you were so interested. Okay, baby. What exactly would you like to know?"

The hot sex in his voice as he emphasized each word made her heart flutter. "Stop that."

He straightened, and dropped the act. "Then let's go."

She tried one last time to make him see reason. "Look, Brent, I don't want you to spend a small fortune on a dress I'll only wear once."

"Give it up, Jen. I'm buying the dress." He held out his hand and wriggled his fingers. "Come on." Jen flopped back against the seat and lifted her chin, absolutely determined to sit firm.

He waited. And waited some more.

A couple of minutes later her shoulders slumped in defeat. The bullheaded man would probably wait all day if he had to. Sighing in resignation, she let him pull her out of the car. Setting a person straight wasn't as easy as it sounded. As soon as he got this dress thing out of his system, she'd try again.

The glass door set in the pink marble archway was emblazoned with a name both world-famous and terrifyingly European. They stepped into the reverent hush of a library discreetly threaded with chamber music. Furniture grouped in refined clusters nestled among the racks—oases of comfort for those who waited for those who shopped. The tall, redheaded goddess in a glorious green silk sheath gliding toward her and Brent was cool sophistication personified.

Good grief, this was light-years away from JC Penney.

"May I help you?" It was quickly and subtly done, but they'd been analyzed and categorized in a single glance, and Jen had been found wanting. She shifted self-consciously.

Brent must have sensed her discomfort, because he squeezed her hand, smiled, and said, "No thanks, we'll just look around."

No doubt stunned by Brent's killer smile, the redhead nodded vaguely and floated off. Jen had a split second to console herself with the thought that all women were apparently created equal when it came to the punch in a Brent Maddox smile, before he dragged her toward the evening dresses.

"Why," Jen muttered, following truculently in his wake, "do you insist on taking me where the hired help act like I have some kind of unfortunate disability? First Henri's, now this place."

Brent looked down at her. "I don't know what you're talking about. What disability?"

"Socioeconomic Dysfunctional Disorder."

"Oh, *that* disability. Don't worry, honey," he said, and winked, "we'll have you rehabilitated in no time."

"Now there's a promise that could keep me awake nights."

He managed to buy her a dress, but she made him work for it. He nudged her past the lack of price tags, prodded her into choosing style over practicality, and nagged her into modeling for him. Emotional blackmail seasoned with a dollop of guilt turned the last trick, and the sleek little black silk number was finally in the bag.

When she'd stepped out of the dressing room to model it, he'd had to clamp his teeth together so his tongue wouldn't roll out of his mouth and down to his knees. There were curves in that dress, and they were curvier than he'd thought they would be.

A night on the town was starting to sound damned good.

Things got a little dicey when Jen found out exactly how much the dress cost, but he hustled her out of the store after her first squeak of surprise. Thankfully, she didn't work up to full-fledged ranting until they got to the car.

"That was the most outrageous piece of retail theft I have ever seen! It was nothing short of highway—" Brent lost her harangue when he closed her door, but picked it up again when he climbed in behind the wheel. "—never heard of anything so . . . so . . . exorbitant. My God, it's crazy, that's what it is!"

"What?"

"What?" Jen looked incredulous. "We just spent more money on a dress than most people spend for a used car!"

"So?"

"So that's ridiculous!" Her eyes were snapping, her cheeks flushed. She was really worked up—and looking good with it. "They certainly have their nerve charging prices like that!" She jiggled the garment bag. "What does this dress have that one from Penney's doesn't?"

As the lone defender of the integrity of Rodeo Drive's boutiques, he offered, "Quality?"

"Quality, schmality." Jen ran her fingers through her hair. "You had no business buying me a dress that cost this much."

Figuring a quick agreement would take the wind out of her sails, he said, "You're right. Buying you that dress was an awful thing to do."

"And the underwear to go with it," she reminded him pointedly.

He rubbed his nose to hide a smile. "Ah, yes. The underwear. I'm a slimeball, all right."

"But did you listen to my objections? Oh, no. You just went right along on your merry way."

Feeling more amused by the second, he suggested, "Maybe you should shoot me."

But the lady wasn't listening. Obviously on a roll, she tossed up her hands. "What kind of people put up with snotty waiters and snooty salesclerks just so they can pay unreasonable prices for food and clothes?" Then she answered herself. "Materialistic people, that's what kind. People with more money than sense."

Brent started the car and eased into traffic. "Hmm. You know, I think I understand the underlying problem here."

"I should hope so."

He nodded slowly. "See, what we're dealing with is a misdiagnosis."

"You'd better believe—" She blinked. "Huh?"

"Seems clear to me. You don't have Socioeconomic Dysfunctional Disorder at all."

She looked lost. "I don't?"

"Uh-uh. I'm afraid the disorder you have is a lot more serious."

Her frown bordered on totally baffled. "It is? What is it?"

"Socioeconomic Attitudinal Disorder."

"Socio—" She shook her head. "Look, Brent, one of us isn't making sense. Maybe you should try again."

Pulling up at a red light, he turned to smile at her. "Well, to put it in layman's terms . . . you're a snob."

They probably heard her gasp in Pasadena. "A *what?*"

"You heard me, a snob. S-N-O-B, snob."

"I am not!"

"Are too."

"Am—" Her teeth clicked together. He watched her lips move in a silent count to ten before she asked, somewhat reasonably, "Why do you think I'm a snob?"

The light turned green, and he started the Jag moving again. "Look, Jen, you're a nice, sensible person."

"Now, why don't I think you mean that as a compliment?"

Bright woman. "Unfortunately, it's been my experience that nice, sensible people often come equipped with nice, narrow points of view."

"Are you saying I'm narrow-minded?" Obviously the thought had never occurred to her.

"If the shoe fits."

"And you think it does?"

"Well, yes—based on what I've seen so far. You judge everything you see by your own small-town standards."

"I'm not judg—"

"Sure you are. Everybody *you* know buys their clothes in department stores, so the rest of the world should too. Nobody *you* know spends the money to eat *haute cuisine*, so anybody who does is spoiled, shallow, and materialistic. Right?"

Jen squirmed. "I didn't say—"

" 'Materialistic people, that's what kind. People with more money than sense,' " he quoted.

She blushed. "Oh, uh . . . I guess I *did* make a few rash generalizations. I apologize. Let's just forget I said anything."

"No, no, that's not how rehabilitation works. We

have to move past denial—get to the root of your problem."

"The root of my problem?" She closed her eyes briefly. "Oh, Lord."

"Hmm. Okay, let's look at this logically, using me as an example."

"Honestly, Brent, this isn't necessary."

"Sure it is. And you being a teacher and all, I figure we'll make this like a little quiz. Okay, listen up. I have money. I came by it legally, if not by the honest sweat of my very own brow. Does this make me a bad man—inherently immoral?"

"Oh, for Pete's sake, of course not."

"Very good, Jennifer. The next question is a two-parter and multiple choice." He ignored her strangled protest. "Having money, shouldn't I be able to spend it any way I want? Or should I maybe: A) give it all to the ASPCA; B) bury it and hope it goes away; or C) shred it for mulch?"

"Don't be silly; you can do whatever you want with your money, as long as you don't spend it on me."

He nodded. "Unless I want to. Now to the crux of the problem: Do you think I patronize places like Henri's to impress people like you?"

She chuckled weakly. "Not unless you're a lot dumber than you look."

"Thanks—I think. So I'm not out to make a big impression. Maybe I wanted to intimidate you."

"I force sixteen-year-old boys to read Elizabeth Barrett Browning. Intimidation? I don't know the meaning of the word."

"Good point. So we can rule out intimidation as a possible motive. That leaves putting on airs. Do you see me acting the *crème de la crème* to your skim milk?"

Exasperated sigh. "You're very nice. Hardheaded, stubborn as all get-out, but nice."

"In other words, I'm a lot like you."

"And I don't have money. Ergo, rich people are just like everybody else."

"See? That's what I like about teachers—they're so smart."

"Gee, thanks. At least you think I'm a smart snob." Then a minute or two later: "I guess I *should* thank you for the dress."

It amazed him that she could repent and sulk in the same breath. Being a wise man, he didn't laugh. "You're welcome."

Evidently, spending his money still didn't sit well with Jen. On the contrary, it seemed to ruffle her feathers but good. Not having run into that particular attitude before, Brent didn't quite know how to handle it.

Buying things for women had become more or less a lifestyle choice. Most of the ladies in his life liked getting presents. Hell, most of them more or less expected it—not that he minded. Much. But buy an expensive dress for Jen Casey, and you lit a fuse that burned fast and hot.

As far as she was concerned, his money was more an irritant than anything else. That being the case, he realized suddenly, if Jen ever said she loved him, it would be the real McCoy. His heart gave a quick jump, which he just as quickly quashed. Jen wasn't his type, and he wasn't ready for the real McCoy.

Still, it was nice to know women like her existed.

If he ever decided to take the matrimonial plunge, he'd look one up.

Jen tapped his shoulder. "You know, all that power shopping gave me quite an appetite."

He flashed her a grin. "Me too. What would you like to eat?"

"Anything I want?"

"You name it."

Her eyes narrowed. "Anywhere I want to go?"

"It's your call."

"Okay."

"Okay, what?"

"Okay, I know where I want to go."

"Where's that?"

"McDonald's. Us snobs just live for their french fries."

Was this the face of a snob?

Jen leaned over the peach marble counter and peered into the bathroom mirror. Turning her head to either side, she examined her profile. Not a whole lot of nose there. Had she been looking down it at other people? Turning it up at things she knew nothing about?

Absolutely.

"Oh God, I *am* a snob," she groaned. Well, a reverse snob actually. "But a snob by any other name," she muttered, "is still a real jerk." Grimacing in self-disgust, she flipped off the light and trudged into the bedroom.

Tucking the hem of her T-shirt into her shorts, she padded over to the bed. She sat down, sneaker in hand, and stared thoughtfully at the sunny window.

When had she become a judge of books by their covers? She treated poems better than she'd treated Brent and his class. At least with poems she looked beneath the surface, trying to find the heart. Didn't people deserve at least that much consideration?

Maybe that was the key: From now on she'd treat everybody she met with the same respect she'd give a Shakespearean sonnet. Accept each as individual and unique, keeping in mind the commonalities of form and the fact that the surface elements were usually the least important.

Unfortunately, Brent had one heck of a surface, and it kept getting in her way. Rich, sexy, and sophisticated tended to dazzle a woman; getting past all that so you could see the rest of the man took real willpower, but she was determined to try.

Despite the fact that he hadn't said more than a couple of hellos to her in high school, Jen had always felt she'd known him. In a peewee town like Donnerton people got to know each other through sheer propinquity, something like social osmosis. The boy she'd known then had been cheerful and friendly. Cocky and confident without being obnoxious.

Well, aside from being rich as Croesus these days, he hadn't changed all that much. She'd told him so at dinner last night, but now, for the first time, she understood how true it was.

He could laugh at himself. The man who had every right to arrogance accepted being under his housekeeper's thumb with wry good humor, and took her own clumsy jabs to his ego with grace and a grin.

On the debit side, he was obviously used to having things his way and exercised more than his share of high-handedness when it came to getting them there.

Not only that, he gave the phrase *generous to a fault* new meaning. Unfortunately, that generosity attracted just the kind of mercenary women Brent claimed not to want in his life. Why couldn't he see that?

The temptation to be the one to finally open his eyes was a strong one. And that was dangerous, because the urge to improve a man was one of the most seductive known to woman. If there was one thing Jen didn't need from Brent, it was more seduction.

Which brought her to The Kiss.

It hadn't been her first kiss—good God, she *was* twenty-eight, after all—but it had been the first to leave her warm and restless. She'd . . . wanted. Really wanted. That kind of wanting usually ended with fevered moans between satin sheets in candlelit rooms. Which would have been fine, if she were the type for a brief, blistering affair.

No such luck.

Jen knew she couldn't intensely want a man in a physical way without eventually wanting him just as intensely in other ways. Emotional ways. Caring-and-sharing and stay-with-me-forever ways.

Brent Maddox wasn't anybody's idea of a stay-forever kind of guy.

In the final analysis, Brent was good people. Very sexy good people. She liked him, and enjoyed being with him. She also wanted to kiss him again. If she listened to her common sense, she couldn't. She wanted to save him from himself. If she listened to her common sense, she wouldn't.

Feeling almost unbearably sad all of a sudden, Jen tugged on her sneakers, tying the laces in double knots so they wouldn't trip her on the tennis court. Every once in a while common sense really sucked.

FIVE

"Where in the hell are you?"

"Malibu."

Silence. Then: "What in the hell are you doing in Malibu?"

"I'm with Brent."

"Oh, fine. I'm imagining fates worse than death, and you're off in Malibu with some . . . Brent? You don't know any Brent."

"Brent Maddox."

Candy's snort was eloquent. "Okay, Jen, where are you *really?*"

Through gritted teeth: "I am in Malibu with Brent Maddox."

The next pause ended with, "You're serious."

"Dead serious." Jen smiled tightly into the receiver. "You remember that letter you triple-dog-dared me to write?"

"Uh-huh."

"Well, because of that letter, Brent showed up on my doorstep Tuesday night."

"He did?"

"*And* dragged me out to dinner."

Candy went from shocked to intrigued in a nano-second. "*Dragged* you?"

"Don't get smart."

"Okay, you went to dinner with him. How did you get to Malibu? Did he *drag* you there too?"

Heaving a disgruntled sigh, Jen admitted, "He dared me."

"Ahhh. That explains everything. What, exactly, did he dare you to do?"

"Stay with him for a week. And don't get any sleazy ideas. He wants to get to know me. That's all!"

"Mm-hmm."

"What's that supposed to mean?"

"Oh, nothing." Candy's airy tone had Jen grinding her teeth. "Now let me get this straight. You're in Malibu with a rich, gorgeous hunk of male."

"That's right."

"And . . . this is bad?"

Jen thought about the dress, the gala, and The Kiss. "I don't know."

"Look, I don't see the problem. Most women, myself included, would kill for a week with Brent Maddox. Why don't you just relax and enjoy yourself?"

"Because I'm not most women, and Brent Maddox is dangerous."

"Now, Jen, dangerous isn't necessarily a bad thing. A little risk can enhance—"

Good Lord. "You're certifiable."

"Hey, you're the one complaining about a dream vacation with studmuffin. Come on, you can handle it. It's only for a week."

Jen hesitated. "You think so?"

"Absolutely." Candy sighed lustily. "A week with Brent Maddox. Girl, that's next door to heaven. What have you been doing?"

"Shopping. Tennis at his—" She was interrupted by a disgusted oath.

"You made Brent play—I'm sorry—tennis?"

Jen pouted. "He didn't seem to mind chasing the ball . . . unlike some people I could mention."

"So chivalry isn't dead. What'd you do besides run the man ragged around the edges of a tennis court?"

"Nothing yet, but we're supposed to go out on his sailboat."

"Oh, God."

"I won't lower the boom on him." She hoped. "Good grief, Candy, you act like I'm a catastrophe about to happen. I'm not that bad."

"Are we forgetting the Rollerblade incident?"

Jen's eyes narrowed dangerously. "*We're* trying. And if you want to hear about Brent, you'll change the subject."

"Oh. Right." Candy drew a breath. "Sooo . . . does he look as yummy in person as he does in his pictures?"

That was more like it. "Yummier."

Candy groaned. "You lucky dog! Give me details. Get into the spirit here, girl!"

"Right." Actually, it was easy. She dropped back on the mattress, pictured Brent, and cruised straight into soft-and-mushy. "Well, his eyes are dreamy, so blue you could drown in them. Honest to God, Candy, I think I did." Twin sighs were exhaled over the wires. "His hair's thick and wavy and tumbles down to his collar. He's tall, and built like a—"

"Yeah. Ain't he just?"

Jen smiled dreamily. "His voice is Sean Connery and Richard Burton rolled into one. And when he kissed me—"

"Hold it right there!" Candy barked. "He kissed you? Brent Maddox kissed you?"

Plummeting back to reality with a wince, Jen said, "Forget it."

"Oh, no you don't. Did he, or did he not, kiss you?"

"Yes."

"Oh, my God. He kissed her! So?"

"So what?"

Impatience crackled over the line. "So how was it?"

Well, why not tell her? Jen grinned smugly. "On a scale of one to ten? An easy twenty."

"Lord have mercy!"

"Hmm."

"You know, this could be the start of something big."

Jen sobered immediately. "Not a chance."

"You can't say—"

"I do say. You may be right. Maybe I should relax and enjoy my visit. But Brent's lifestyle isn't for me. I'm not a lap-of-luxury kind of person."

"Lap-of-luxury is a learnable skill."

"I don't think so."

"But—"

"Besides, what would a man who's dated some of the world's most beautiful women want with me?"

Candy was nothing if not loyal. "Don't sell yourself short. He kissed you."

"Natural inclination. Brent's what they used to call a rake. He probably kisses every woman he goes out with."

"Now you're selling *him* short."

Of course she was, but what else could she do? She already itched to change him and had the hots for him. The combination had self-preservation alarms clamoring. Emotional distance was crucial, which meant she had to remember Brent's reputation with women. It was for her own benefit as well as Candy's that she said, "Don't plot any happily-ever-afters."

Candy wasn't ready to give up. "If he's not interested, why did he dare you to stay with him for a week?"

Good question. "A whim, maybe. But as far as I'm concerned, it's just a 'dream vacation with studmuffin.'"

"You can fall for a studmuffin—and vice versa."

"But not for a man who plays all day every day."

"God, Jen, you are such a snob."

Jen's shoulders sagged. "Yeah. I'm working on it."

"And you gave him an A?"

Jen scooped up a last spoonful of chocolate mousse. "Why not? It was a very good poem."

Leaning back in his chair, Brent shook his head. "Teachers sure have changed since we were in high school. I don't think old Mrs. Kratzmeyer would've appreciated a poem comparing her teaching technique to Chinese water torture, no matter how well it was written."

Jen chuckled warmly. "That's a fact. She was a holy terror, wasn't she? Remember the way she used to make us stand up to face the class and read love sonnets out loud? A fate worse than death. At least, it seemed that way back then."

"Actually, whenever I think of Hilda Kratzmeyer, I remember wondering about her breasts."

His confession earned him a choked gasp and a wide-eyed look of disbelief. "Hilda Kratzmeyer was at least sixty years old!"

"Yeah, but I still wondered. I mean, did she have any?" He contrived to look innocent and earnest. "I probably wouldn't have given her breasts—or lack of them—a second thought if she hadn't worn her belt up around her armpits." He grinned when Jen clapped her napkin over her mouth to muffle a burst of laughter. "Well, didn't you ever wonder about that? It sure looked uncomfortable."

"That's awful. Is that the kind of thing adolescent males think about during class? Good Lord, I'm glad I can't read their minds. I'd never be able to face a classroom full of teenagers again."

If those high-school boys could see her now, he mused, wearing that sleek blue jumpsuit, candlelight throwing hints of red into her hair and softening those big eyes to dark, bedroom brown, they'd be weaving fantasies hot enough to singe their eyebrows. He sure as hell was.

He should never have kissed her. Ever since that kiss, every nerve in his body had gone hypersensitive, so everything about her brought on a surge of lust. The sound of her voice. Her scent. Even her button nose. A man was in bad shape when the crinkle of a button nose got him hard.

Until now cute women had never turned him on. He couldn't remember the last time he'd lost the battle to keep his hands to himself, but Brent figured he'd run up the white flag about an hour ago.

Since jumping Jen's bones on the dining-room table would be really bad form, he opted for conversation. "I can't quite picture you riding herd on twenty-five or thirty adolescents. How do you do it? A whip and a chair?"

"Or a small-caliber automatic. Actually, if you can get them to forget that reading poetry is an assignment, they dive right in."

"Ah, a blind leap into Byron."

"Exactly."

"You really do love it, don't you?"

She grinned. "Yep. Makes quite a statement about my mental health, don't you think?"

What he thought was that he envied the hell out of her. It bothered him on some new, irksome level that he lacked that kind of dedication—to anything. Would he feel that passionately about his chosen career if he had one?

"You two want more coffee?" Crampton materialized at his elbow and stood stolidly next to his chair, pot in hand.

"Not for me, Althea."

"Me, either. That was a wonderful meal, Mrs. Crampton."

Brent was amazed to see his housekeeper's usual unrelenting glower crack into what he assumed was a smile. His startled gaze flew to Jen. How had she done that?

"Well, thank you. I'll tell Cook you said so." Crampton's face had already settled back into its familiar scowl by the time she turned to Brent. "You going to need anything else?"

"No." He closed his eyes briefly, then opened them again. Crampton was her normal, dour self. Even her apron looked rigid. Maybe he'd only imagined the smile. "No, that'll be all for tonight."

"All right, then." And with a squish of her rubber soles, she was gone.

He swiveled back around to stare at Jen. "How'd you do that?"

"Do what?"

"How'd you make Crampton Bligh smile?"

Jen laughed. "You don't really call her that, do you?"

"Not to her face. Do I look like I have a death wish? She'd probably take me out with a copper-bottomed sauté pan."

He liked the way her lips twitched right before she smiled—it made him want to kiss her again. Like this was news. He'd spent all of last night and the biggest part of today wanting to kiss her. Kissing Jen, and doing lots of other delicious things to Jen, was quickly becoming an obsession.

"Crampton never smiles at me—or anybody else, for that matter." He paused. "Unless you count that last time Mitch and Carla came for dinner."

"Mitch and Carla?"

"Jake and Carla Mitchell. I've called him Mitch since college days. He and his wife are among the chosen few—Crampton actually *talks* to them."

"But Crampton Bligh? She can't be that bad."

"Worse. The woman's a heartless tyrant, the Terminator of domestic service. And when her spring-cleaning hormones kick in . . ." Brent gave an exaggerated shudder. "Let's just say the crew on the *Bounty* were better off with the captain, and leave it at that."

Slipping into a credible imitation of Long John Silver, he chortled, "Aye, runs a tight ship, does Crampton Bligh. Fact is, mate," he added, rising from his chair, "we'd best clear the decks and let 'er swab 'em down, or she'll have us walking the plank afore lights-out."

"Where are we going?" she asked—a little suspiciously, it seemed to his sensitive ears.

"I thought we'd take a walk along the beach."

"Oh." She looked at Brent's outstretched hand the way a doe might look at a hunter packing a .22. "I don't know if that's such a good idea."

"I always take a walk after dinner," he lied. "It's great for the digestion. And you can't visit Malibu without beach-walking. I think there's a city ordinance against it. Besides, my beach is special."

"*Your* beach?"

"Yep." He waggled his fingers invitingly. "Come on, live a little. The ocean's beautiful this time of night."

"Well . . ." Her stare dropped back to his hand. Slowly, she placed her own in it, and he let out the breath he hadn't known he was holding. *Gotcha!*

It was a picture-perfect summer night, soft and warm. Like the woman walking beside him, he thought, sort of poetically. Waves tumbled in under a star-strewn sky to dissolve in a silvery froth against the sand, their rhythmic whisper both hypnotic and deeply sensual.

"Oh, Brent, it's beautiful."

He glanced around, then down at her. For some

reason, he felt as if he were seeing both the woman and the beach, really seeing them, for the first time. "Yeah," he agreed gruffly, and swallowed. "Beautiful."

"Wait." She pulled him to a stop and perched on one foot to pull off her sandal. "I want to go barefoot. Sand's fun when you're barefoot. With shoes it's a nuisance."

Seconds later she had her sandals dangling from one hand, and his hand clasped in the other. They strolled silently for a few minutes, then she peeked up at him. "You said you met Mitch in college. Which college?"

"Princeton."

"Oh, you're an Ivy League playboy," she said, but her impish grin wouldn't let him take offense. "What was your major?"

"Business administration." His lips twisted wryly. "Not my first choice, but it seemed like the thing to do at the time."

She cocked her head. "What was your first choice?"

"Architecture. When we inherited I decided a degree in business administration would come in handy as far as managing the family fortune."

"Did it?"

"No. The way it's set up, everything pretty much takes care of itself."

"Hmm. It must have come as quite a surprise—inheriting all that money, I mean. The papers said you didn't even know your cousin."

"Three times removed, cousin by marriage, to be exact. Never laid eyes on the man. It took the estate lawyers almost five years to track us down, and two days to convince Dad the whole thing wasn't some practical joke. It was a surprise, all right."

She slowed to a stop, and her gaze met his, suddenly intent. "And your life is better for it? You're happy?"

Disconcerted by the question, he cocked an eyebrow. "Of course I'm happy," he answered automatically, then annoyed himself by wondering if that was strictly true.

"Good." Smiling brightly, she dropped his hand to scamper up the beach, laughter trailing in her wake. "Oh, this is great!" She darted toward the water, squealed when it lapped over her feet, and skittered back. "It's cold."

Brent stared after her, shaken by her question and his answer, but mostly by the doubt it had raised in his own mind. He was also confused by the concern he'd glimpsed in her eyes. He watched her, and for some reason, his heart started to hammer, hard and fast.

She was only playing, enjoying the sand and water. She wasn't trying to seduce him. But he was being seduced. His mouth was dry, and he ached for her. Only for her, damm it!

Flinging out her arms, she laughed and turned a quick pirouette. *That does it*, he thought grimly, and started after her. *Just how much is a man supposed to take, anyway?*

"You know, I've never—" She gasped when he grabbed one of her arms to spin her into his. Her eyes were dark pools of uncertainty as she gazed up at him. "Brent?"

He didn't answer, mostly because he wasn't sure he was capable of speech. Instead, he skimmed a hand up her back and fisted it in her hair, gently pulling back her head. His gaze devoured her face and homed in on her luscious mouth. Then his lips did the same.

She stiffened as if she wanted to pull away, so he tightened his hold and deepened the kiss, spiraling his tongue deep. A second later he heard something hit the sand. Her sandals, he realized dimly.

Some vague, still-functioning corner of his mind wrestled with the question of how cute could get him hotter with one kiss than gorgeous had with a whole lot more. And she was innocent. God help him if she ever figured out what she was doing. Then she raised herself on tiptoe and gave him her tongue, and his brain shut down all together.

"Oh, sweetheart." He strung a line of kisses down her throat. Her head dropped back and she arched closer in invitation—an invitation she probably didn't realize she was making. Either way, Brent accepted. In one long sweep, his hands ran down her sides to her thighs and brushed back up to settle on her hips. He tugged, fitting her snugly against his erection, and they both moaned.

"Brent, we shouldn't—"

His brain had shut down, but his instincts were in perfect working order and smothering her protest was an involuntary reflex. Dragging his mouth back up her neck, he recaptured her lips and thrust his tongue deep, over and over, until she draped pliantly against him. Then his hand slid up to cup her breast. He swept his thumb across the tightly beaded nipple, tasted her gasp, and caught her when her knees buckled. He lowered her to the sand and followed.

"I want you," he growled. Her eyes flared—in panic or desire?—but he was already sliding on top of her, settling between her thighs. He nudged his aching groin against her heat.

She started to shake her head, but his fingers plunged into her hair, gripping her skull to stop the motion. Just a kiss away, her rapid breaths fanned his lips. "And you want me, Jennifer. Don't you?" He pinned her with a look that dared her to lie.

She stared up at him, looking wild, wanton, a little scared. Her pulse fluttered visibly at the base of her throat. "I . . ." She licked her lips, dragging his eyes back to her mouth. "Yes," she whispered.

He left one hand tangled in her silky hair while the other traced down her throat to the zipper that ran between her breasts. He found the tab and tugged gently. Material parted to reveal satiny skin. His fingers slid into the opening to dance across the lace of her bra. She strained up into his touch, and he almost exploded. Christ, she was so damned responsive!

"Brent—" She whimpered when his fingers edged under the lace. "Brent, I'm getting wet."

"Oh God, baby, I hope so." He ground his mouth down on hers and closed his fingers around her nipple, tugging gently. Her arms clenched around his waist, her hips jerked, and she shuddered.

"Brent, I'm *really* getting wet. I think the tide's coming in."

It took a minute for her words to sink in. He shook his head to clear it, raised up on his elbows, and looked down at her. "What?"

"The tide's coming in."

He glanced back over his shoulder. Water eddied up under their legs. Common sense told him they should move, but his frantic body didn't give a damn about time or tide or anything else. The only movement his overcharged libido was interested in was the thrust that would put him inside her.

Desire won hands down, and he lowered his lips to hers again, murmuring, "Don't worry, sweetheart, if it was good enough for Burt Lancaster in *From Here to Eternity*, it's good enough for me." Nipping at her bottom lip, he rubbed against her.

Evidently, his wasn't the only body with a one-track mind, because she purred and gyrated with him, one of her feet sliding up the back of his leg. He got just a taste of what it would feel like to have her legs wrapped around him before she sighed and murmured regretfully, "Yes, but Burt was in Hawaii. This water's *cold.*"

Dropping his forehead to hers, he battled the childish urge welling up inside him. Grown men simply did not cry like babies just because things didn't go their way. Not even if the way things went left them hot, hard, and horny as hell.

"Okay." He touched a kiss to the end of her nose, then forced himself to climb off and help her to her feet. His wistful gaze ran over her kiss-stung lips and wildly tangled hair. He might cry after all.

Shooting an unhappy look over his shoulder, he wondered if a quick dip in the Pacific would put out the fire in his blood, because he'd bet his last million Jen wasn't going to suggest they go back to the house and burn up the sheets.

An hour later Brent lay on his back in his lonely king-size bed, hands stacked behind his head. Frustration was eating him alive; the old-standby cold shower hadn't come through for him this time.

He contemplated the shadows shifting across the ceiling, and swore ripely. Sometimes, being right was a real pain in the ass.

SIX

There comes a time in every woman's life when she's forced to pause and reflect. A time to take stock of her circumstances and make decisions about the future. A time to face reality head-on and deal with it.

And a time to get the heck out of Dodge.

It was, Jen admitted dispiritedly, about that time.

Last night she'd had a very close call. The thing that worried her—scared her right down to her toes, actually—was the fact that she couldn't decide which upset her more: The fact that there had been a call to begin with, or the fact that it had only been a *close* one.

Sighing, she dropped her head against the sun-warmed windowpane and closed her eyes. Be honest, Jen, if only with yourself. You wanted to make love with him. But if not for the grace of God and the Pacific, you would have.

Making love with Brent would have been easy, frighteningly easy. The scene-that-could-have-been played itself out in tantalizing detail behind her closed eyelids.

Arms wrapped around each other, they could have strolled back to the house, pausing to kiss and caress along the way. Intimate murmurs and the soft laughter of soon-to-be lovers would have filtered through the spacious rooms and high archways, up the wide staircase to the enormous master bedroom.

Then undressing one another slowly in front of the bank of windows overlooking the Pacific, exploring each other's body by touch and moonlight while passion continued to build gradually, layer upon heated layer. Falling onto that massive bed, arms and legs tangled, to writhe atop the forest-green spread. Yes, it would have been easy.

That was the scene-that-could-have-been. The scene-that-was hadn't been nearly as romantic. It had involved a lot of shying away from his touch, babbling inanely, and practically running up the beach on her part, and grim, resigned silence on his. As soon as they reached the house, she'd blurted a good night and ducked into her room like the panicked, virtuous maiden she still was. Even now, in the bright light of day, she didn't know whether she was disappointed or glad about her still-snowy status.

Yes, making love with Brent would have been easy. Stopping, on the other hand, hadn't been. As a matter of fact, stopping had been darned near impossible.

Jen still wasn't sure how she'd managed to call a halt when every single nerve ending in her body had been quivering for completion. One long, ineffective bath, two purloined chocolate-covered éclairs, and eight hours of restless tossing and turning later, her thwarted hormones were still sulking.

But even more disturbing than the ache for physical consummation was the craving for emotional completion. Single-handedly battling raging hormones was child's play compared with combating her heart's desire, and her heart wanted her to give herself to Brent. Didn't her heart have more sense than that? Brent was a confirmed bachelor.

Obviously her heart wasn't thinking straight.

It was time to make tracks, dare or no dare.

With another sigh, she opened her eyes and straightened away from the window. "Darn the man! Isn't it bad enough that he has a face and body to die for and more sheer magnetism than the North Pole? Does he have to be so . . . so . . . wonderful?"

Feeling aggrieved, she stalked to the closet, flung open the door, and started pulling out her clothes. "I don't want to leave. It's *his* fault I have to.

"The least he could do is be the obnoxious play-jerk he's supposed to be. Who asked him to be so blasted nice, anyway?" she fumed, tossing everything on the bed. "Like he has to be generous and have a great sense of humor on top of everything else? Talk about overkill!"

Eyes flashing, movements jerky, she grimly folded one item after another. "And does he have to kiss like that?" she muttered. "Turning a woman's bones to mush and her mind into Silly Putty?"

God only knew she resented it, but even the memories made her feel hot. Whirling, she stormed back to the closet and yanked a suitcase off the shelf, too incensed to remember that neither closet nor suitcase was hers.

"Stay with me, he says. Get to know me, he says." Her lips twisted derisively. "Oh, he makes it sound so innocent. Like he doesn't know he's the kind of man some poor, dumb woman could start falling in love with."

Panic froze her in place. Love? Just the thought of it catapulted her into full fight-or-flight mode. Fortunately, she was already mid-flight.

Slinging her clothes into the suitcase, she mumbled, "Okay, calm down. Anything that can start can stop just as easily. And right this minute!"

If she had started to fall in love—not that she admitted to any such idiocy—then she'd just stop. Resolute, she closed the clasps and swung the case off the bed, striding purposefully toward the door.

Distance. All she needed was a little distance. Better yet, a lot of distance. Only fools believed absence made the heart grow fonder. Absence was going to save her sweet patootie.

Brent could just drop his all-too-perfect self in his own private stretch of ocean. She was outta here. She was going to march down these stairs, straight out that front door, get into her car and . . .

Her determined stride faltered, slowed, and finally stopped. It would be tough to get into a car that was roughly two hundred miles away. She huffed in self-disgust. And thanks to her hurried packing job night before last, all the cash she had to her name amounted to that measly twenty she'd tucked in her wallet, which wouldn't make bus fare.

When she finally noticed the expensive piece of luggage dangling from her right hand, her head dropped back and her eyes closed. "The only place you're going, Jennifer Marie, is out of your ever-loving mind."

No problem, she decided, straightening her shoulders. Brent was the one who'd brought her here in the first place. Brent would just have to take her home again.

For some stupid reason, the idea of Brent taking her home had tears threatening. Her grasp on the suitcase's handle tightened. "Oh, no. No crying. You're not in love yet. And you're not going to be." What she was going to be, was gone. She lifted her chin and started down the stairs.

Althea Crampton appeared out of nowhere and planted herself at the foot of the stairway. The term *immovable object* flashed through Jen's beleaguered brain as she came to a forced stop on the bottom step. "Going somewhere?"

"I'm leaving."

The housekeeper's eyes narrowed. "What do you mean, leaving?"

"Well, I . . ." Suddenly feeling like a felon in a police lineup, Jen shifted her weight. "I have to . . . that is . . . I thought I'd better go home."

"Why?"

The tone—blunt bordering on belligerent—had Jen squirming visibly. "Something's come up."

"What?"

The graceful acceptance of social lies evidently wasn't one of Althea's strong points. "Just . . . something." Althea stared expectantly, and at length. The silent pressure was too much, and Jen bristled defensively. "Because I want to, all right?"

"Why?"

Temper overcame embarrassment. Jen's expres-

sion took on what Candy liked to call her Francis-
the-Mule Look—chin up, jaw set pugnaciously.
"Look, Mrs. Crampton, I have things to do at home."

Black eyes bored into brown, and Jen suddenly
knew what a very small bug felt like when skewered
on a very large pin. "Baloney. You're scared, that's
what you are."

Barely managing to keep the *How did you know?*
behind her teeth, Jen tried for cool and aloof. "I don't
know what you're talking about."

The housekeeper didn't buy it, but pointed an ac-
cusatory finger in Jen's face. "You're running away."
Straightening, she folded her arms across her ample
breasts and shook her head. "I thought you had more
brass than that."

What was going on here? Why would Althea
Crampton care whether or not she left? *And why do I
feel ashamed because I want to?* "It's not a matter of—"

Crampton turned away. "You run home with your
tail between your legs if you want to, but mark my
words, missy, that boy needs you. Be a real shame if
you let him down." She glanced over her shoulder.
"Nice suitcase."

Too astonished to be embarrassed at being caught
Vuitton-handed, Jen watched Brent's housekeeper
stalk off. *Brent needed her?* A fascinating idea, even if it
didn't make any sense. What could *she* possibly have
that Brent Maddox needed? An extensive knowledge
of English grammar? Intimate knowledge of the Romantic poets?

"Needs me. Right. And the Invisible Man needs a
photo ID." But she couldn't quite dismiss the idea
when she turned down the hallway to go looking for
him.

She found him stretched out on a chaise on the spacious patio overlooking the ocean, and groaned silently. He *would* have to be wearing nothing but a ragged pair of cutoffs. Jen looked to heaven. *Give me a break here, will you?*

Thanks to the morning sun and his own coloring, he looked cast in gold. He shifted, muscles flexing smoothly as he raised his arms languidly to stretch like a big, sinuous cat. That quick, the heart rate it had taken her all night to level lurched back into double time. Boy oh boy, did she ever have to get out of here!

"Brent?"

He turned his head. His blue-lagoon eyes blinked sleepily. Then his lips curved, slowly, into that devastating smile. "Good morning." Even his voice sounded catlike—a raspy, sexy purr that brushed goose bumps down her arms. And the way he was looking at her . . .

Okay. It was technically impossible to actually feel a gaze run over you, but she felt it anyway. First on her face, then on her lips, her neck, and her breasts. And wherever his eyes touched, heat followed. Waves of it. Her stomach tightened in response.

When he saw the suitcase, his eyes lost their sensual glow, sharpening before they snapped back to her face. Still, his question was surprisingly mellow. "Going somewhere?"

She almost gave in to a desperate laugh. *Away from you and temptation just as fast as my legs will carry me.* "I'd like you to take me home today."

He swung his legs off the chaise and sat up. Now more than ever, he reminded her of a cat—a lion. Jen found herself looking into the unblinking stare of a predator, facing the complete stillness before the killing lunge. "I thought we agreed that you'd stay for a week."

"I changed my mind."

He stood, and she took a step back. "Welshing, Jen?" he asked softly. Way too softly. She swallowed.

She didn't care for his terminology, but had to admit it was accurate. Her shrug was half discomfort, half faux-cool. "If that's what you want to call it."

"That's how I see it. Why? I didn't think you'd turn deadbeat, sweetheart."

Inwardly, she winced. But unable to deny the charge, she kept her mouth shut.

"Know what I think?"

Don't ask. But she couldn't help herself. "What?"

"I think you're afraid of what *almost* happened on the beach last night."

Jen frowned. How did he know? How did Althea know? Did everybody in the world know? Maybe she had *frightened virgin* stenciled across her forehead. "I am not afraid," she lied. Unfortunately, she didn't lie often enough to do it well.

He stepped closer, and she edged away. "You're afraid right now. You're scared I'll kiss you again."

Thank God for righteous indignation. "Oh, no you don't! You promised not to kiss me, remember? And you call *me* a welsher! Ha!"

Shaking his head, he laid a thumb across her lips. "I didn't promise not to kiss you, honey. I promised not to do anything you didn't want me to do." His thumb rubbed gently. "And last night you wanted a hell of a lot more from me than a kiss." His voice deepened. "And that's what's got you spooked, isn't it? The way you went wild in my arms. You're not afraid of me—you're afraid of yourself. And of what you damn well know is going to happen between us."

The man was a walking, talking triple-dog dare. Unable to move or look away, Jen fought the newest riot he'd incited among her nerve endings. She wanted to moisten her lips, but his thumb was in her way. And given the frustrated-hunter look in his eye, she didn't think licking his thumb would be smart.

Afraid? Darn right, she was afraid! Like she'd told Candy, the man was dangerous. All he had to do was touch her, and . . . Darn right, she was afraid!

But rather than admit the truth, she flew back to her original point, just like a homing pigeon. "I'd like to leave as soon as possible."

His jaw flexed. "No."

Jen blinked, because he couldn't have said what she thought he'd said. Unassuaged lust had probably thrown off her hearing. "What?"

"I said no. I'm not taking you home today. You agreed to spend a week with me, and I'm holding you to it." As if that ended the discussion, he strode past her into the house. "Are you ready for breakfast? Personally, I'm starving."

Head tilted to one side, Jen stood where she was, waiting for things to start making sense. Unfortunately, thirty seconds of intense concentration didn't change the situation. She still wanted to go home, and Brent still wasn't going to take her. As soon as the facts registered, she got mad. Turning on her heel, she raced inside.

"Brent." She caught a glimpse of him as he disappeared around the corner. "Brent, wait. I want to talk to you."

His back retreated right on up the stairs. She and her temper charged after it. "You come back here!"

"I have to get a shower before breakfast." He ducked into his bedroom.

Undaunted and as angry as a swarm of wet hornets, she chased after him, latching onto his arm when he would have disappeared into the master bath. Digging in her heels, she clung like a limpet when he tried to pull away. "You take me home!"

"No."

"You can't just say no!"

"Sure I can." He looked down at her and smiled thinly. "Watch. No."

She gaped then shut her mouth with an audible click. "Okay, fine," she snapped, and flung away his arm. "I'll call Candy. She'll come get me."

"Oh no, you don't." This time, *he* caught *her* arm. Hauling her over to the door, he closed and locked it. He snatched the suitcase out of her hand, swinging it out of reach when she made a grab for it. "You're staying right here. For one week. *We had a deal, lady!*"

For one giddy moment she wondered if *right here* meant in his bedroom. Her mouth went dry at the prospect.

Common sense quickly reasserted itself, bewilderment following closely on its heels. "I can't believe you're trying to force me to stay here. You're acting crazy! What's wrong with you?"

He dropped her arm. "Nothing's wrong with me," he muttered. "You're the one who's trying to renege on our bargain."

Still confused, she scooped the bangs off her forehead. "Okay, you're right. I am trying to renege.

What I don't understand is why you'd make such a big deal of it."

Shooting her a harassed look, he backed toward the bathroom, taking her suitcase with him. "I'm not making a big deal of it. I just think people should do what they say they'll do, that's all."

"But—"

He stopped, eyebrows snapping together. "But nothing. You said you'd stay, and you're staying. End of story."

Her own temper started to reheat. "I write my own stories, buster. I don't have to stay if I don't want to. And I don't want to."

"You have to."

Exasperated, she tossed up her hands. "Why?"

"Because." He started backing away again. He was nearly through the door.

"Because?" Jen rolled her eyes. "Well, that's certainly as clear as mud. Because." She sneered, and started toward him. "Because why?" she all but shouted.

"Because I need you!" he yelled back, and stopped her dead in her tracks.

She gawked at him. "You need me?" It sounded just as far-fetched coming from him as it had coming from Althea Crampton. But the fact that he'd said it at all knocked the wind out of her. "For what?" she asked faintly.

For a split second he glowered like a disgruntled little boy. "Damned if I know!" he growled. "But I've got until Tuesday to figure it out!" was punctuated by the slam of the bathroom door.

❖————————❖

"I'm hiding out in the bathroom, holding a woman's clothes hostage."

Brent shook his head. Pathetic. Thank God, his friends couldn't see him now.

But what the hell else was he supposed to do? She wanted to leave him. His lips thinned with determination. Jen Casey wasn't going anywhere just yet, and that was that.

Had he really told her he needed her? He hadn't meant to say it—mostly because he thought it might be true. It scared him spitless.

It also left him bare-assed vulnerable. And feeling stupid to boot, because he didn't know *why* he needed her. The least she could do was hang around until he figured it out.

Besides, there was unfinished business between them. Last night they'd started something, and for the sake of his sanity he meant to see it through.

Feeling the woman turn into a wild thing in his arms had been a heady experience. Jesus, she was so damned hot! A fire in his blood. And he was going to light that fire again. Light it and stoke up a blaze that would fry them both. Incineration or bust was his motto from now on.

But first he had to convince Jen to stay.

He scowled at the door. Except for the fact that she could let herself out anytime she wanted to, locking her in his bedroom had been a pretty good idea. His grin was quick and fleeting. Locking her in his bedroom was a great idea; it gave rise to all kinds of interesting fantasies. Too bad they didn't make locks the way they used to, so that person needed a key to get out. He'd have her right where he wanted her then.

He angled his chin. He still had her right where he wanted her. She didn't have a car, and probably didn't have enough money to get herself home. Otherwise, she would have flown the coop under her own power instead of asking him to take her back. Glancing at the suitcase next his feet—his suitcase, he noticed—Brent smiled in satisfaction. Snatching her clothes had been a smart move.

Jen couldn't go herself, and he wouldn't take her. That left her friend Candy. Alarmed, he stared at the door. She'd threatened to call for a ride home. Never mind the fact that the estate was isolated and surrounded by a privacy wall. If this Candy was half as stubborn as Jen, she'd find a way in. His heart lurched. What if Jen was calling her right now?

Spinning around, he lunged for the wall phone next to the shower and yanked the receiver out of the cradle. No symphony in the world could match that sweetly reassuring buzz of a dial tone. She hadn't called anybody. Yet.

And she wasn't going to. Feeling smug, clever, and just a tad foolish, he unplugged the headset and shoved it into a drawer. There. No calls today, in or out. She was staying.

Now all he had to do was make her like the idea. The problem, he decided as he stepped into the shower, was that he'd pushed too hard and too fast. He reached for the soap and started to lather his chest.

Chemistry between a man and a woman could be a powerful thing. The chemistry between him and Jen was more explosive than the usual, ranking somewhere between nitroglycerin and a hydrogen bomb. Things heated up so fast, he forgot everything but the driving need to take her, including the fact that she was a virgin. Damn! No wonder she was scared. She probably felt like the innocent lamb to his ravening wolf.

Tilting his face up into the spray, he told himself to slow down and back off a little. One way or another, if he didn't give her some space, she would bolt. He wouldn't be able to keep the phone off the hook indefinitely, nor would he be able to keep her locked away like some princess in a tower.

He didn't want her locked away. He wanted to take her out and show her a good time. He wanted to discover what it was exactly that she had in her life that he lacked in his. To do this, he needed to see her react naturally in as many different situations as possible. That wouldn't happen if she was obsessed with leaving, so he'd back off.

For a while.

But he'd eventually win her over, he promised himself. Sliding back the opaque glass door, he reached for a bath towel. It would take time and patience, but he'd have her. Jen Casey was going to discover passion in nobody's arms but his.

As he wrapped the towel around his waist he felt the featherlight touch of apprehension. Where had all this . . . possessiveness come from? This obsession with one particular female? His brows drew together. She was just another woman. Wasn't she?

No, he admitted reluctantly, and picked up his razor, she wasn't. She was different. Somehow, in a very short time, she'd become much more important than the other women he'd known. Too important maybe. Why else would he fly into a blind panic just because she said she wanted to leave him?

He felt it again, that slight, warning tingle along the spine. *Watch your step*, it seemed to say. *She's getting to you.* Well, he'd watch his step but good from now on.

It was okay to like Jen. It was vital to make love with her. It was crucial to learn whatever it was she had to teach him.

But at the end of their week he'd let her go so they could both get on with their lives. Of course, she'd always hold a special place in his heart—they were going to be lovers, after all. And thanks to her, his life was going to be more rewarding and meaningful.

Someday, in the distant future, when he was ready to settle down and get married, he'd look for somebody just like her.

His train of thought jolted to a stop. *When* he was ready? *Somebody just like her?* Jesus! Where did that come from?

He glanced at the razor in his hand, then laid it carefully on the counter. It seemed like a good idea. The way his hands were shaking, he was liable to cut his throat.

But then maybe he already had. He pictured the crazy-cute woman in his bedroom. The woman he wanted more than he wanted his next breath.

And tried to ignore the internal voice of doom whispering that his caution had come too late.

SEVEN

Jen teetered to a halt just outside the hacienda's front door. Her teeter went with the ankle-breaker heels the saleswoman had insisted she needed to go with this black excuse for a cocktail dress. She halted because of what she saw on the curve of the circular drive.

"What's that?"

Brent glanced at the gleaming gray vehicle then back at her, one golden eyebrow raised. "A car."

"It's a limousine!" She pointed an indignant finger. "With a chauffeur!"

Lips pursed thoughtfully, he turned to study the Mercedes, and the man stationed at the back passenger-side door. "You know, I think you're right."

Her stomach twisted nervously. "I thought we were going in *your* car."

"This *is* my car," he answered calmly, and taking her elbow, propelled her forward. "Evening, Donald."

"Good evening, Mr. Maddox."

The driver was young, clean-cut, and muscular. In his immaculately tailored dark blue suit he looked every inch the cool professional. Until Jen noticed the twinkle in his green eyes and realized Donald was making a valiant effort to stifle a laugh.

She was acting like a moron again.

She pressed her lips together. It might block the next idiotic statement that tried to slip out without her brain's permission. Her brain had other things to do, like concentrating on how to get into the car without baring five or six inches of thigh. The five or six the dress bared all by itself were plenty.

There wasn't much fabric between snug, stapless bodice and abbreviated hemline. A second skin had nothing on shantung silk; Jen felt as if she were wearing a very slinky postage stamp.

After giving the logistics some thought, she sat sideways and swung both legs into the car simultaneously. Tugging futilely on her swatch of skirt, she hoped Brent planned to get in through the other door. Sliding across the seat would have embarrassing sartorial repercussions. "Why do women dress like this, anyway?"

"Uh . . . well . . ." Glancing up, she caught Brent with his eyes glued to her legs. Donald too. Turning her head, she hid a flustered blush and smile. So *that's* why women dressed this way.

Male throats cleared in a flurry. Donald closed her door and hurried around to open the other one for Brent. A few seconds later they were off in a plush gray cocoon equipped with all the comforts of home: bar, telephone, and television set. Determined not to act the fool any more than she already had, Jen gawked but kept her mouth shut.

"Would you like a drink?" Thinking his voice sounded huskier than usual, she turned to look at him, but couldn't see his face because he was fiddling with the bar.

"You remember our tennis game?"

His hands stilled while he slanted her a quizzical look. "Yeah."

"Well, as it happens, my athletic ability is second only to my drinking ability. In other words, when alcohol and I mix it up, alcohol usually wins. I think I'd better keep my seat on the wagon so I don't embarrass you tonight." She gestured toward her feet. "Besides, these shoes are risky enough when I'm sober. I wouldn't want you to have to fashion a splint out of swizzle sticks."

His eyes dropped to the collection of black leather straps that crisscrossed her feet, then climbed slowly up her legs. The warmth started in her toes and crawled up after his stare. By the time his glittering blue gaze reached her face, *something* in the car was ready to overheat. And she was it.

He took a deep breath and shifted his stare to the smoky glass between them and Donald. "You'll be all right. And you could never embarrass me."

"I'm certainly going to try not to." Resisting the urge to fan herself, she groped for composure and prayed that he was right about her social skills. Ever since he'd mentioned attending this gala charity benefit, she'd been battling a bad case of nerves. Okay, not nerves exactly . . . more like mind-numbing panic.

Tonight she was going out into his world—all the way out. Like on a ledge. Moving in wealthy and exalted circles, meeting the cream of society. *Oh, God.*

"Did you say something?"

"Uh, no."

If she had any sense at all, she'd jump out at the next traffic light, shuck the shoes, and hotfoot it back to Donnerton.

Sliding a secret glance at her escort, she suppressed a groan of self-disgust. Sense? Not her, brother. Not anymore.

The old, sensible Jen wouldn't be caught dead in a limousine with a hunk. The old, sensible Jen didn't wear sexy-socialite clothes. The old, sensible Jen would avoid what promised to be the most intimidating function of her life. Heck, only yesterday the old, sensible Jen had been determined to leave!

It had only taken three words. Three little words, and she mutated from a perfectly reasonable woman with a healthy instinct for self-preservation into putty in a man's hands.

I need you.

Unbelievable as it was, he'd said it. And because he hadn't been able to explain what he meant, she *did* believe him. Which made absolutely no sense at all. But because she believed him, she was staying. Amazing.

She sneaked another peek. He looked magnificent in a tux, but based on what she'd seen so far, the man looked good enough to eat in anything he put on. She ruthlessly blocked the image of what he would like with nothing on. She was in enough trouble as it was.

The intermittent glow of streetlights briefly gilded his hair and illuminated his strong profile. He was, she repeated silently, absolutely gorgeous. And he needed her. How could she refuse to stay?

And how badly would she be hurt *because* she'd stayed?

Ah, well, but regrets and heartache were for another day. Probably tomorrow. Tuesday at the latest. Right now she had other things to think about. "Where are we going?"

His start was slight but unmistakable. What had he been thinking? Was he having second thoughts about bringing her along? She certainly had second thoughts about coming along.

"I told you. It's a benefit for a pet project of mi— uh . . . for Hope Away from Home. The foundation wants to set up houses in different parts of the country where seriously ill children and their families can stay cost-free when they travel away from home for specialized treatment."

"A pet project of yours."

He shrugged, managing to look both nonchalant and mildly embarrassed. "I've done some work on it."

Jen shifted to face him. "I remember reading about that somewhere. According to the article I read, you've done more than *some* work on it. The whole thing was your idea."

Now he looked really embarrassed. "What whole thing? The concept of the halfway house didn't exactly originate with me, you know."

"I know. But—"

"A lot of people work for the foundation. You'll be meeting some of them tonight."

If he wanted the subject closed, she'd oblige. For now. *"Where* will I be meeting them?"

"Beverly Hills. The Windham Bel Lage Hotel."

"Oh. That should be interesting."

Her sudden burning desire to look out the window was camouflage for a wince. *That should be inter-esting?* Lord, Jennifer!

His fingers curled around her fist, and she started. "Relax, honey, you don't have a thing to worry about." When she finally worked up the nerve to face him, he winked. "This is supposed to be a party, you know, not an execution."

"Easy for you to say," she muttered glumly. "You won't be the one teetering to her doom on killer shoes. But I'll try to keep the party line in mind."

Freezing a smile on her lips, she turned to stare out the window again. Not that she saw anything. They could have driven by a street-side performance of the Chippendales and she wouldn't have noticed.

She was on the verge of falling apart here. What she needed was another pep talk. So she gave herself one.

Okay, Jennifer. Get hold of yourself. You can do this.

No, I can't. I don't belong here. I'm going to mess up and act like a dork.

Where's your backbone?

At home.

Your pride?

Dorks don't have pride.

Knock it off! You're not going to mess up and act like a dork. You're an intelligent woman. A highly educated, professional woman.

A woman who doesn't have a clue about how to behave around people like these. And I am not being a snob!

Of course you're not. But you can get through this evening. All you need is a plan.

It wasn't long before she settled on a five-pronged attack.

Rule Number One: Don't gawk or act like a narrow-

minded schoolmarm. Be polite and nonjudgmental. And remember, you're every bit as good as anyone else.

Rule Number Two: Stand and sit carefully. Above all, don't bend over or you'll reveal both your northern and southern exposures.

Rule Number Three: Avoid alcoholic beverages of any kind.

Rule Number Four: Walk slowly. Don't topple off your shoes.

Rule Number Five: Stay in the background. Avoid attracting unnecessary attention.

Number Five was critical. If she stayed in the background—Brent's anonymous companion, as it were—she wouldn't commit any serious social gaffes. Invisibility was the key to social success.

The car slid smoothly to a stop. Satisfied with her modus operandi, Jen felt reasonably confident when the door opened and she accepted Brent's hand.

Heck, she thought, sliding gracefully out of the Mercedes, *I'll be so quiet and unobtrusive, they won't even know I'm here.*

On her first relaxed breath of the evening, she congratulated herself. Feeling poised and a little smug, she stepped up to Brent's side and smiled.

At least twenty flashes exploded in her face. While she was blind somebody shoved a microphone under her nose.

If she weren't stunned, Brent wouldn't have minded having Jen Casey plastered up against his side, hanging on like a sinner to her last hope of salvation. He'd been having a hell of a time keeping his hands off of her, so he welcomed any excuse to touch her. As a matter of fact, he'd been looking for one.

The tide of reporters surged toward them and her fingers tightened on his arm. He smiled for the cameras but kept moving steadily through the throng, eyes forward. He avoided eye contact with the press because he didn't want to invite or answer questions.

He avoided eye contact with Jen for the sake of his sanity. If he looked at her, he'd haul her into his arms and kiss her within an inch of her three-inch heels. He'd been fighting the urge all night, and he couldn't give in to it now. Jen wouldn't appreciate it if he turned her into paparazzi food.

But damn, she looked great! Her hair was piled on top of her head, exposing the graceful curve of her neck. Brent tried to remember the last time a woman's neck made his mouth water. He couldn't

That outfit wasn't helping his self-control any, either. She'd modeled the dress before, but tonight was the first time he'd seen the full effect. Had it only been an hour ago? One look, and his knees had threatened to buckle. Luckily, he'd been sitting at the time.

By now the pool of reporters surrounded them, eddying and shifting, tossing out questions. He wouldn't have believed Jen could get any closer to him than she was, but somehow she managed to edge nearer.

"It's all right," he murmured, bending down so only she could hear the reassurance. "We'll be inside in just a minute."

Her tremulous smile was brave and strained, and sent his heart on a slow tumble. Foreign and baffling as the feeling was, an undeniable surge of protectiveness rose up inside him. He laid a hand over the slim fingers clutching his arm and gave them an encouraging pat. "Hang on, honey." The doorman and sanctuary waited a few scant feet away.

They almost made it.

"Mr. Maddox, can you tell us who your . . . *companion* is?"

The woman in the chic, ice-blue suit planted herself directly in front of them. Judging from her bold stance and flinty stare, she was about as budgeable as a five-foot-six-inch concrete wall. Recognizing true intransigence when he almost ran into it, Brent stopped. He felt Jen tremble and his smile took on an extremely unpleasant edge. "I'm sorry, Ms.—"

"Dawson. Emily Dawson. I'm with *Celebrity*."

"Right. Well, Ms. Dawson, what was the question again?"

A flicker in the reporter's eyes acknowledged the sharp lick of temper in his voice. "I asked who your companion was." The request lacked the sly insinuation that had tainted it the first time around.

Twelve years of experience had taught him it was best to answer while keeping his reply as simple as possible. "This is Jennifer Casey," he started moving again. "She's an old friend of mine."

They swept through the door before Emily could follow up on his statement. The lobby they entered was luxurious. And quiet.

They were safely ensconced in the elevator on their way to the tenth-floor rooftop garden when the full impact of what had just happened hit him. Brent swore vehemently.

Jen looked up at him. "What's wrong?"

"That was Emily Dawson—from *Celebrity*." Jen's

eyes widened, and he nodded. "It's only a matter of time before she connects you with the Jen Casey who wrote the letter." Brent barely checked the violent oath that rushed to his lips.

"Will that bother you?"

He glanced at Jen. Her hold had loosened fractionally, but he knew she was still uneasy about the evening ahead. "The question is, will it bother *you?* You don't know it yet, sweetheart, but we're about to become extremely public property. Are you going to bolt?"

She frowned up at him. "I told you I'd stay."

"Yeah, but didn't tell me what changed your mind."

"And I'm not going to unless . . . maybe you'd care to explain why you said you need me?" Since he still wasn't sure himself, he shook his head. "Then you don't need to know why I'm staying."

She was wrong, but he didn't know how to tell her that.

Insecure and *woman* weren't words Brent usually used in the same sentence. His discovery of the opposite sex dated back to age fourteen. His ability to manipulate the delightfully complex creatures developed a couple of days later. As far back as he could remember, he'd never doubted his boy-meets-and-gets-girl expertise.

Until now. The words *insecure* and *Jen* went together like bread and butter.

He was feeling the prick of some very nasty pins and needles. Not knowing why Jen had decided to stay, he didn't know how to avoid driving her away. It was a lot like walking backward through a minefield. Blindfolded.

Insecurity was a real bummer.

The elevator doors whooshed open. Brent set his jaw and firmed up his resolve. One thing at a time. She was staying. If she changed her mind again, he'd deal with it. He wasn't going to let her get away.

Gosh, Toto, I don't think we're in Kansas anymore. Now Jen knew exactly how Dorothy must have felt when she caught that first breathtaking glimpse of Oz. The world outside the elevator was every bit as fantastic.

Cognizant of Rule Number Four, she stepped carefully onto the terra-cotta patio, searching her brain for words to describe her reaction to her surroundings. *Holy Ike!* was the best she could come up with.

The rooftop garden was magnificent. Planters exploded with bursts of color, tall ficus and palm trees gathered in clusters. Off to one side lay the glowing rectangle of a swimming pool. The music was jazz and as mellow as the warm night air. In every direction and as far as the eye could see, Los Angeles spread out in a vast sea of winking, flashing lights.

Jen had big-time trouble with Rule Number One when she recognized one of the men chatting near the bar.

Cam Dolan! In the heartthrob flesh! Tall, brooding, and Byronic, from head to toe the surly, unapproachable god of stage and screen.

One of his companions leaned in to whisper something, and Dolan threw back his head to roar with laughter. The transformation was staggering. *Exit Alpha-Male-Sex-God, enter Cute-All-American*

Guy. Jen caught her sagging jaw mid-drop, barely avoiding a rule-breaking gawk.

Just then a leggy blonde drifted into her field of vision. The woman was draped all over a distinguished older gentleman, talking a mile a minute. If the pair had been a sculpture, Jen would have labeled it *Gold Digger with Sugar Daddy.* What expensive trinket was the mistress cajoling from her aging lover? Jen wondered with a blush.

The two moved within hearing range, and Jen heard the blonde say, "I'm telling you, B.C., you've got to stay away from junk bonds. It's a bear market out there. Stop by the office first thing Monday and we'll go over your portfolio."

The mantrap in silver lamé was a stockbroker? Geez! Weren't any of these people what they seemed?

Just then, Terry Masters popped into her head. Rebel-without-a-cause tough, arrogant, and sulky. A bad attitude on the prowl, and one of Jen's favorite students. It had taken weeks, but she'd finally uncovered the gooey center Terry hid under his hard-case shell. I-Don't-Give-a-Damn Terry was a pushover for Dylan Thomas.

Jen looked around and winced guiltily. Her streak of snobbism evidently ran deeper than she'd realized. She wasn't just a snob—she was a compulsive snob.

In spite of Brent's talk and her own soul-searching, she'd made up her mind about these people even before she climbed into Brent's limousine. Heck, she'd probably made up her mind about rich people sometime around the age of four! Rich people were aloof, jaded, and decadent. Pretty and worthless, their antics entertainment for the real world.

Brent and Candy are right. I'm a snob. A nickel-

plated, narrow-minded, small-town snob. Jen straightened her shoulders. No more. She was turning over a brand-new attitude leaf right this minute.

"Brent!"

Ah, her first customer. Determined to see people as they were and not as she expected them to be, she carefully scrutinized the man striding toward them. Using her new, desnobfiscated eyes, she concentrated on looking past the tux—and the brunette on his arm.

An inch or two shorter than Brent, the newcomer was dressed as formally as everyone else, but his fiery red hair was on the shaggy side and slightly tousled, his smile big, friendly, and uncomplicated. She could probably like this man.

Reluctantly, Jen switched her attention to his date—a bigger challenge to her newborn social egalitarianism. But then most women harbored a prejudice against delicate brunettes with faces like Botticelli angels. She pasted on a welcoming smile, reminding herself that envy was both a useless and an unattractive trait.

Brent stepped forward to clap the redhead on the back. Since Jen was hanging on to his arm, she got dragged along for the ride. "Hey, Mitch! How have you been? Carla." He dropped an affectionate peck on the lady's cheek. "You keeping this big lug in line?"

"Of course. I always keep you in line, don't I, Lug, dear?"

Brent shook his head, gazing woefully at Mitch. "How the mighty have fallen. Princeton's original party animal, reduced to sniveling respectability. CEO of Mitchell Electronics and firmly brought to heel by a woman."

"Don't knock it, buddy. Your time will come." Mitch directed a pointed look at Jen.

"Oh, sorry. Mitch, Carla, this is Jen. Jen, meet Jake Mitchell and his wife."

"Call me Mitch." Mitch offered his hand.

Watching hers disappear into it, Jen murmured, "Nice to meet you."

"Like I told you the other night, Mitch and I go back a long way. Hell, we were frat brothers."

Carla nodded. "Not to mention partners in crime, brother rogues, and inseparable troublemakers."

Mitch gifted his wife with a look of mild reproach before turning to Brent. "Didn't expect to see you here tonight."

"Why not? I'm chairman of the fund-raising committee."

"And every other damned committee for every other damned charity in the city. But I thought you were taking some time off. Going back to Donnerburg to get even."

"Donner-*ton*," Jen corrected automatically. She filed away the charity remark, figuring she'd interrogate later. Right now there were so many other interesting things to talk about. Tilting her head, she peered up at Brent. "Get even?"

"Forget it," Brent muttered, glowering at his friend.

But Mitch's affable green gaze had sharpened— and it was currently aimed at Jen. "Donnerton. Right. How did you know that?"

"I live there."

"Yeah?" Jen could almost see the connection click. "Your last name wouldn't happen to be Casey, would it?"

Oh, lord. Had everybody on God's green earth read that stupid letter? Suddenly her shoes felt absolutely fascinating. Which was probably the reason she stared at them as she mumbled, "Yes."

"Ahhhh. You're *that* Jen." He chuckled. "I have to tell you, lady, you've got a real way with words."

She didn't want to, but Jen forced her gaze away from her shoes, up to their faces. Mitch was grinning. Brent was glaring at Mitch. Carla dug an elbow into her husband's ribs. "Would somebody mind telling me what's going on?"

Naturally, it was too much to hope that Mitch would keep his mouth shut. "Sure, hon. Haven't you figured it out yet? Ms. Casey here wrote the letter."

"Letter?" Carla looked from Jen's blush to Brent's scowl.

"Yeah." Mitch waggled his eyebrows. "You know, *the letter.*"

"What—" Comprehension dawned in Carla's hazel eyes. "Oh, *that* letter." She gazed at Jen with real respect. "You do have a way with words."

Jen wanted to sink through the floor—all ten of them. "Thanks."

"Yep, that was some letter, all right." Mitch delivered a hearty slap to Brent's back and earned yet another dark look. "Caused quite a stir for our boy here."

Brent was blushing. In spite of her embarrassment, Jen felt her lips quirk. Never mind that the letter had caused quite a stir for her too. For the first time since their reunion, she had the upper hand. She decided to keep it for a while. "So he tells me." Her eyelashes fluttered innocently. "I didn't mean to cause you any trouble, Brent. Really."

An animal noise rumbled in his throat. "I'll just bet you didn't."

Mitch rocked back on his heels. "Guess you're here about that remedial instruction, huh?"

So much for the upper hand. "No, I—"

"Jake." The warning in Carla's voice was clear. Mitch, of course, ignored it.

"You could have him write on a blackboard, five hundred times. *I will not—*"

"Mitch. Old buddy." Brent laid a companionable arm across his friend's shoulders. "You wouldn't want me to have to wrap your tongue around your neck, would you? Be a shame to ruin such a nice tie."

"Well . . ." Mitch pretended to consider.

"Behave yourself," ordered Carla, "or you can sleep on the couch tonight."

Mitch looked hurt. "The couch is four inches shorter than I am. I'll get a crick." Faced with his wife's unrelenting stare, he sighed dramatically. "Okay, okay, I'll back off. But I didn't get to ask her the part about teacher conferences."

"You are such a pain," said Carla.

At the same time Brent said, "God. Come on, let's go get ourselves a drink." He towed Jen toward the bar.

Mitch ambled along, Carla by his side. "So what do you teach in Donnerton, Jen? Creative writing? Ouch!" He looked down at his foot, then scowled at his wife. "That hurt!"

"I certainly hope so," she returned sweetly, and turned to Jen. "What *do* you teach, Jen?"

Preoccupied with avoiding a broken ankle as she tried to keep up with Brent, Jen muttered, "High-school English."

If the darned man didn't slow down, she was going to hurt herself. Fall on her face or some less dignified body part. And in this dress, getting back to her feet would give the hometown crowd a show they'd never forget.

"Slow down," she said. Thankfully, he did.

"What made you decide to come for a visit?" asked Carla.

Stupidity wasn't a socially acceptable answer, but Jen couldn't come up with another. She was relieved when Brent said, "We started talking about old times when I went back to Donnerton, and I invited her to come down for a while."

"Oh. Well, how long are you staying?"

"A few more days."

They reached the bar, finally, and Jen let out a silent breath of relief. All the fine, small bones of her feet and ankles were still intact.

Carla ordered a stinger. "And is Brent showing you a good time?"

"Well," drawled Jen, suddenly amused, "he did take me shopping on Rodeo Drive. It was quite an experience, I can tell you."

Mitch raised an eyebrow. "Was it?"

"Are you kidding? Have you ever been in those stores? My God, they—"

Brent interrupted with a pointed, "What would you like to drink, Jen?"

Oops. Was the newly reformed Jen Casey about to launch into a ringing denunciation of ostentatious consumption? Considering her audience, that would have been unforgivably tacky. But if Brent hadn't blocked the diatribe, her foot would be firmly entrenched between her flapping gums.

She made a mental note. *Thank Brent for saving you from yourself.*

"Jen? What would you like?"

"Oh, club soda, please."

"Club soda? Are you sure? They have a nice Chenin Blanc."

It's probably very tasty, whispered her palate. *Rule Number Three,* insisted common sense. It wasn't until she glanced around and found everyone, including the bartender, staring at her that she realized she'd mumbed the reminder under her breath.

Clearing her throat, she reiterated firmly, "Club soda."

Of course Brent, the dirty dog, knew exactly why she wanted to avoid alcohol. His eyes danced with mischief as he turned to order.

"Don't drink?" asked Mitch.

Not without grim repercussions. But she couldn't say that, either. She settled for a simple, "No."

Brent handed her the soda with a devilish lift of one eyebrow. She ignored the latter and sipped the former.

Out of the corner of her eye, she watched him lift his Scotch and water. Out of the same corner of the same eye, she watched a graceful hand tipped with long, bloodred nails slip between her and Brent. She watched it caress his wrist and crawl up his arm with proprietary familiarity.

A cloud of French perfume drifted in like a noxious fog. Out of the aromatic mist came a feline, feminine purr, followed by the most astounding words.

"Brent, darling, I thought you'd never get here."

EIGHT

Rule Number One didn't stand a chance—Jen gawked for a full thirty seconds. Luckily, nobody noticed, because all eyes were trained on the latest arrival.

Jen had never seen anything like it in her entire life.

The woman was tall, five ten at least. Her hair—coiled in a thick, lustrous chignon—was jet black, her eyes a lighter blue than Brent's. Struggling to remain unbiased and objective, Jen told herself the glint in those eyes was probably intelligence. Ten minutes ago she would have labeled it malice and greed, but having learned her lesson, she was through with labels. Besides, the woman had a face that could launch the entire Pacific fleet. What did she have to be bad-tempered and covetous about?

Jen was the one who should feel bad-tempered and covetous. After all, she was only standing next to that body; the other woman was in it.

It was a body men would talk about with leers and

elbow nudges, drawing hourglass shapes in the air. A body they would describe in terms of small-scale construction done in brick. Full breasts, a narrow waist, and sleek, womanly hips. And it was wrapped up—barely—in the Mother of All Dresses.

Certainly there was fabric somewhere. But wherever it was, it was sheer and flesh-toned, hugging every dangerous curve and hollow. Overall it looked like someone had sprayed sequins and beads in strategically placed bursts directly onto the woman's creamy skin from neck to ankle, concentrating on her . . . Jen's eyes widened. *Oh, my.*

This was no mere woman. This was a glittering goddess, capable of bringing any man to his knees in abject supplication—and enjoying it.

"Hello, Vanessa." It might have been wishful thinking, but Jen thought she detected a note of resignation in Brent's voice. "I didn't expect to see you here tonight."

Still caught in the grip of awe, Jen watched Vanessa raise up on tiptoe, her ruby lips on a collision course with Brent's mouth. At the last second he turned his head and she grazed his cheek instead.

Pouting slightly, Vanessa chided throatily, "Now, darling, you know I wouldn't miss your little do."

Jen blinked. The first faint twinge of emotion pierced her stunned detachment. *Darling?* That was the second time the woman had called him that. Jen's temper stirred and heated. *Little do?* she thought, revving up. If this woman knew Brent half as well as she pretended to, she'd know Hope Away from Home was important to him. Who was this bimbo, anyway?

There was no mistaking the hunger and possession in Vanessa's eyes, or the fact that it winked out like a light when she turned to Mitch and Carla. "Jake, Carla. How nice to see you again." Jen imagined dead trout would be greeted with more warmth and enthusiasm.

The Mitchells returned the frost with a deep freeze of their own. "Vanessa." Mitch offered a curt nod. Carla didn't offer the time of day.

Jen decided she could really learn to like Carla.

Vanessa's blue eyes narrowed vengefully at Carla's slight, but her practiced smile didn't slip a notch. It was still clamped on her lips when she finally turned her head to look at Jen. The temperature in that icy gaze plummeted another fifty degrees. "Aren't you going to introduce me to your little friend, Brent?"

Evidently, like Gulliver in Liliput, Vanessa saw the rest of the world in the diminutive relative to herself. Like Brent's fund-raiser. *And me*, Jen fumed silently. Of course, next to this . . . this . . . *Amazon*, she probably did look small. In more ways than one.

Jen decided she could really learn to despise Vanessa.

"Vanessa Coulton-Brandenburg, this is Jennifer Casey. Jen, meet Vanessa. An old . . . friend of mine."

Only Jen saw the annoyed flicker in Vanessa's eyes. But all four of them heard her sexy chuckle. "Yes, we're old friends, darling." Her ice-pick gaze drilled into Jen's skull as her talons traced up Brent's sleeve. "Very *close*, very *dear* old friends."

Point taken, Jen thought as a light red mist tinted her vision. *Nobody has to hit me over the head with a two-by-four*. She just wished she *had* a two-by-four.

An arrested expression crossed Vanessa's face. "Casey? Now, where have I heard—" All of a sudden her eyes lit with amusement and relief. "Oh, yes. The letter-writing high-school teacher. How sweet."

The condescending harpy. Sweet? This woman wouldn't know sweet if it bit her on her overblown—

"Brent, darling, I've been wanting to talk to you."

Darling again. Okay. It was painfully obvious that Vanessa Coulton-Who's-Her-Face considered Brent private property. It was just as obvious—and twice as painful—to acknowledge that he probably had been once upon a time. But there were two things wrong with the current scenario.

First of all, the woman wasn't nearly good enough for him. Brent needed a warm, sensitive woman who understood him. A simple, unpretentious woman. Not some overpriced, underdressed snob.

Secondly, judging by the annoyed expression on his face, Brent considered the relationship history. This, of course, was very good news. Jen didn't ask herself *why* it was good news, it just was.

Unfortunately, Vanessa obviously hadn't gotten the message. She wasn't ready to give up on Brent. Jen might have felt a teeny trace of sympathy if it hadn't been for the mercenary look in Vanessa's eyes. Or if Vanessa had shown any interest at all in the things that were important to Brent. After all, to have him, then lose him would break a woman's heart.

Why, it would be almost as bad as never having him at all.

The other woman—and that's the way Jen already thought of her—insinuated herself between Jen and Brent. She sidled up next to him, and any compassion Jen might have had went up in smoke.

When Vanessa's fingers trailed up Brent's lapel to toy with the ends of his hair, Jen saw red. More than red. She saw red, green, and all the other colors of the rainbow in jagged starbursts.

When Vanessa crooned, "Darling, I've missed you," a small atomic bomb detonated somewhere inside Jen's skull. Perfectly appropriate, because war had just been declared.

Luckily for him, Brent chose that moment to shift away from the clinging Vanessa. Given Jen's current mood, he might have been elected first casualty otherwise. Taking advantage of the minute space he'd managed to put between himself and the female barracuda in the Versace, Jen stepped neatly into the breach.

She was so mad she forgot to totter on her shoes. She even forgot to worry about her risqué dress. Bold as brass and twice as sassy, she tucked herself cozily under his arm, ignoring his quick, delighted grin.

The smile she sent Vanessa could have sliced bone. Cutting this glossy parasite off at the knees was going to be one of life's real pleasures, and Jen didn't doubt for a minute that she could do it. Granted she lacked the other woman's experience and more obvious . . . ammunition, but thanks to daily skirmishes with a classroom full of teenagers, her psychological warfare technique was razor sharp.

Bringing down Vanessa would be a piece of cake.

"I'm so glad to meet you, Vanessa," she enthused. Her opponent's eyes widened and turned wary. Good. The first rule of mind games was keep the enemy off balance.

Next Jen turned a warm gaze on Mitch and Carla, who were looking nothing if not bemused. "I want to get to know all of Brent's friends."

She had to hand it to the man in question, he

caught on quickly. "And I want all my friends to get to know you, too, sweetheart." Relief and an inexplicable smugness tinged his voice. He gave her shoulders a squeeze not lost on their audience. Jen was pretty sure she heard Vanessa hiss.

"I know!" All innocent excitement, Jen beamed up at him. "Let's invite them over for the weekend. I'm sure Althea won't mind."

Vanessa looked nonplussed. "*Althea?* You and that . . . that battle-ax are on a first-name basis? She talks to you?"

"She's such a dear," murmured Jen fondly. Brent gave a muffled choke. She patted his back. "What do you think, Brent? Can we have your friends over? We have room, don't we?"

Over Mitch's snort and Carla's chuckle, she caught what sounded like a snarl from Vanessa. "*We?* Do you mean to tell me that you're staying with Brent?"

"Staying with him?" Jen managed to blush prettily. At least it felt pretty. "I guess you could put it like that."

"Relax, sweetheart. Lots of people live together nowadays," offered Brent.

"Live . . . together?" Vanessa's sophisticated veneer cracked like thin ice. "You're living together?"

How she achieved the air of casual intimacy, Jen had no idea. Maybe acting was in her blood.

But she slid her hand up Brent's chest and inside his tuxedo jacket as if she did it every day. She let her eyes drift up and lock with his as if they'd locked gazes a thousand times.

Unfortunately, the act backfired on her. Touching him, feeling his heart accelerate under her palm, and

having him return her torrid look—with interest—
almost had her blowing her lines. Hanging on to lu-
cidity by a frayed thread, she struggled to keep the
show on the road. "Yes," she murmured, a little surprised by the husky, loverlike quality of her own
voice.

Brent's hand came up to cover hers, pressing her
palm against his warm chest. His smile hinted at special secrets and shared ecstasy, and sent her pulse
rocketing straight up into the stratosphere.

"We can invite them another time, okay? Right
now I'd rather have you all to myself."

It was the oddest thing. The sounds of music and
laughter faded completely away. All of a sudden pre-
tense was forgotten. Vanessa was forgotten. Carla and
Mitch were forgotten. While she stared up into his
eyes everyone else in the world just . . . disappeared.

The universe contracted, shrank right down, until
it consisted of only the two of them.

She couldn't move, and she couldn't look away.
She couldn't speak. Heck, she couldn't even breathe.
Most of all, she couldn't avoid the truth when it
smacked her right between the eyes.

Dear God. She wasn't *starting* to fall, she'd fallen.
Hard. Heaven help her, she was in love with the man!

Well hel-lo, Green-Eyed Monster!
She was jealous! It would be rude, not to mention
hazardous to his health, to release the smug laughter
trapped in his chest. But he wanted to. Oh, how he
wanted to!

Jen was actually jealous!
Thank God.

Mentally, Brent punched up a triumphant fist. A strange reaction, because jealous women didn't usually turn him on. Of course, cute virgins weren't supposed to turn him on, either.

But not only did jealous women fail to turn him on, they usually left him cold. A jealous date was embarrassing and irritating—except when she was Jen. On Jen, green looked good.

He'd been mad enough to chew glass when Vanessa first showed up. Right this minute his feelings toward the woman waffled between grudging gratitude and a heartfelt wish that she'd get the hell out of his life.

Okay, the two of them had gone out for a while. They'd even been to bed a few times. But taking Vanessa Coulton-Brandenburg any further than bed was, and always had been, out of the question.

She was a beautiful, rich, avaricious piranha. Two years earlier she'd off-loaded husband number three. Women like Vanessa didn't care to have their men spaced too far apart, so the lady was on the prowl for fresh meat and a hefty bank account. Brent didn't intend to be anybody's prime cut. Six months ago he'd broken off with her. Unfortunately, Vanessa was pitbull tenacious—partly because she wanted him, but mostly because she hated being rejected.

He would have bet the hacienda the sleek Ms. Coulton-Brandenburg would make mincemeat out of Jennifer Casey in any given confrontation. And he would have lost.

He'd been all set to play the gallant protector when Jen suddenly turned tigress, complete with very long, very sharp claws. For the last five minutes she'd been using them to sweetly, politely slice her opponent into long, bloody strips.

He really ought to thank Vanessa. If she hadn't come along, he might never have seen the jungle cat in his demure little teacher. What a woman!

Just now, though, Jen was staring up at him, looking like somebody had clipped her with a Louisville Slugger. He understood, of course. Their interpersonal chemistry was acting up again, and it played merry hell with all rational thought processes.

He was having a little trouble in that area himself. Jen's when-can-we-go-home-and-do-it-again-baby routine was driving him out of his mind. If the cute, innocent Jen was hard to resist, the sultry, seductive Jen was electrifying. One of these nights he was going to tap into that voltage.

But since Jen was obviously temporarily out of commission, he'd carry the ball for a while.

Tearing his eyes away from her pale face, he sent a crooked smile and a plea for understanding to their fascinated audience. "You know how it is, don't you? We need some time alone right now. To get to"—*strategic, insinuating pause*—"know each other."

Vanessa looked ready to eat raw meat.

"Sure, we understand," Mitch said soberly. Brent wondered if the straight face was costing Mitch as much as it was him.

"Of course." Carla smiled. She cooed up at her husband, "We remember those early days together, don't we, darling? And the nights?"

Message received.

"This is all very touching," Vanessa drawled snidely, "but I'm afraid I have to be going."

She shot Jen a look that was half fury, half bafflement. Apparently Vanessa knew she'd been routed, but didn't understand how it had happened without a shot being fired. The woman was obviously incredibly dense. She smiled cuttingly. "Good-bye, Brent. Ms. Casey. It's been . . . interesting."

Jen seemed to give herself a little shake. She blinked, drew in a deep breath. Evidently having pulled herself together, she turned to launch her parting shaft.

"Oh, I'm so sorry you can't stay." She actually looked disappointed, but then she brightened. "Maybe we could get together for lunch sometime."

Vanessa did your classic double take. "I doubt it. My schedule is very hectic."

Looking enraged and more than a little shell-shocked, she treated them all to a curt nod before she stalked away.

Deafening silence flowed into her wake.

Brent knew he was going to lose it. He had to hold back, because he wanted to avoid a nasty, public scene. All he had to do was wait until Vanessa was safely tucked away in the elevator. He could do that. Maybe. The pressure in his chest was building to a critical level. If he didn't relieve it soon, he was going to explode.

Vanessa reached the bank of elevators. She pressed the down button and stood, back rigid, waiting for the doors to open.

Hold it. Hold it.

The car arrived. Vanessa stepped regally inside and swept gracefully around to face front.

Not yet.

The door started to close.

Just a second more.

She was gone. Brent chanced a glance at Mitch. The tightly clamped lips and beet-red face did him in. He and Mitch erupted at the same time. They laughed until tears rolled down their cheeks.

"Stop it, you guys, people are staring." But with a gulp and a hiccup, Carla joined in.

"What—" Jen sucked in a shaky breath between chuckles and wiped a tear off her cheek. "What are we laughing about, anyway?"

Her question set everyone off all over again.

"God," Brent finally wheezed, "that was really something. I've paid big bucks to see performances on Broadway that weren't as good."

"Yeah." Handing his wife a handkerchief, Mitch gazed at Jen with unbounded admiration. "You are really something, Jen Casey."

"I am?" Jen smiled a beguiling, cat-that-ate-the-canary smile. Brent's gut knotted in immediate response. "Yeah, I am something, aren't I?"

Carla nodded. "I'll say. You know, I've always wanted to see that witch get what was coming to her, but I didn't expect her to get it from Snow White. I don't think I've ever seen anybody dissected quite so . . . well, graciously. She never knew what hit her."

Jen looked peacock proud of herself. Swamped by simultaneous surges of lust and tenderness, Brent wanted to sweep her into his arms and off into the night. He wanted to carry her to his bed and lay her down. Kiss her. Everywhere. Touch her. Everywhere. He wanted to make love with her until Southern California froze over.

He sighed silently. Soon. But not tonight.

He'd pushed too hard the night before last, and

she'd come close to running away. He wasn't going to make the same mistake twice. She needed time to come to terms with the way things were going to be between them.

Thank God the physical attraction between them was potent. Jen's performance tonight proved there were other factors at work, too. He already knew she wanted him physically. If she cared enough to be jealous on top of that, she wouldn't be able to resist him—or herself—much longer.

He was going to have her. Soon.

"Comfortable?" The strong arm around her shoulders tugged slightly. Obligingly, Jen scooted closer.

"Mm-hmm." Snuggling her head up under his chin, she let her eyelids drift down. The car was so quiet, the ride smooth. Except for the occasional sweep of light from outside, they were wrapped cozily in darkness.

"I had a good time. It wasn't quite the ordeal I thought it would be." She hadn't made a fool of herself. Hadn't acted like a dork. Well, not after the first few minutes anyway.

"You expected an ordeal?" His voice was rich with suppressed laughter. "Honey, you've got to get out more. Income taxes are an ordeal—parties are supposed to be fun. So what did you think of my friends?"

Wrinkling her nose, she said, "Okay, so I liked them."

"Quite a surprise, huh?"

She smiled. "You win. I'll admit the people at the

benefit were very nice. Just as nice, in fact, as people back home. They're just packaged fancier."

Of course, like every barrel, this one had its rotten apples, and Lady Vanessa was Queen Winesap. That was one encounter, Jen thought complacently, wherein the rube from the sticks had come out on top.

"You're learning, sweetheart."

"Well," she murmured modestly, "education *is* my life."

And her latest lesson left her with some heavy-duty thinking to do. Life had its turning points, and she'd come to one. She didn't want to veer off in the wrong direction.

It wasn't exactly love at first sight—in a way, she'd known him for years—but it was darned close to it. And while the speed with which it had happened left her breathless, it wasn't cause for doubt. She was in love with Brent Maddox. All-the-way, head-over-heels, once-in-a-lifetime in love.

The charming rogue she'd fantasized about in high school had grown up to be a remarkable man. She loved the cocky guy-next-door who lived behind the glitzy image and tons of money. She loved the man who worked hard for worthy causes, but refused to talk about his contributions. She loved everything about him. Period.

Should she tell him?

A man like Brent probably collected heartfelt *I love yous* from scores of women. He'd have no way of knowing that *she'd* never said it before, at least not to anybody outside her family. She didn't think she could stand it if he dismissed her feelings as infatuation, or worse yet, simply accepted them as his hunk's due.

Either one of those reactions was likely to turn her into a raving maniac. It would be a shame to rip out all that beautiful blond hair during a psychotic rage.

Suppose she didn't tell him?

Keeping her feelings bottled up wouldn't be fair to her, or to him either. After all, this was the man who was looking for a woman who loved him and not his money. Didn't he deserve to know he'd found one? Wasn't unconditional love the greatest gift one person could give to another?

Finally, if she didn't admit her feelings, how was she going to find out how he felt about her? Oh, he liked her well enough, or he wouldn't have wanted her to stay with him.

He said he needed her—a staggering admission, even if he wouldn't tell her why.

And—the memories sent heat rushing up under her skin—he wanted her. There was certainly no doubt about *that*. Or about the fact that she wanted him just as much.

Yes, she should tell him she loved him. Trouble was, she wasn't sure she'd be able to get the words out of her mouth. Just the *thought* of telling him made her lips numb, turned her tongue to lead, and made her throat close up.

Maybe, she thought as her heart fluttered and started to speed, she could *show* him. She managed to swallow, but her throat made a dry click.

Oh, boy.

Was she ready for this? Could she go through with it?

And if she did, would Brent realize she wouldn't give her body if she hadn't already given her heart? According to Candy, men could be awfully dense about things like that.

If Brent was dense, she could end up with nothing but a broken heart and a handful of memories.

But wouldn't memories be better than nothing?

The drop to the bottom line was terrifying, because the bottom line was this: She'd never loved a man before, but she loved Brent. What's more, there wasn't a doubt in her mind that she'd love him for the rest of her life, even if he never returned her feelings. If there was going to be a first time, she wanted it to be with him. Even if the first time turned out to be the last time.

And maybe, just maybe, the first time would lead to a lifetime of other times.

Her heart pounded like a kettledrum. She felt light-headed, almost unbearably excited. She was going to do it. The next time Brent grabbed her and kissed her, she would grab and kiss him right back. Then she'd run her hands up under his shirt and over that broad, hairy chest. Follow that golden line of hair all the way down his abdomen, clear to his—

Whoa! Surreptitiously wiping her sweaty palms on her skirt, she decided to save the rest of the fantasy for later. She didn't want to attack him right here in the backseat of his limousine. Donald would get the surprise of his life when he opened the door.

Not right now, but soon. She was going to make love with Brent Maddox. Soon.

Maybe even tonight.

The possibility had her swallowing again.

Oh, boy.

NINE

He was in bad shape. Something had changed.

When they left the hotel, Jen had climbed into the car to curl up against his side like an affectionate kitten. All of a sudden she seemed totally relaxed around him, and eminently touchable. Her head lay on his shoulder and every once in a while she'd kind of . . . nuzzle.

The woman was driving him crazy. Not knowing whether or not she meant, or even understood, the signals she was broadcasting only made it worse.

Even if she didn't know what she was going to him, Brent could see all his good intentions about giving her time start to smolder. A few more minutes of cuddling, and they'd go up in flames.

Uh-huh. He was in bad shape.

The car swept up the drive, gliding to a halt in front of the house. It was both a relief and a disappointment to be home. Just when Donald stepped out to open the door, Brent felt the butterfly brush of lips against his neck. His head snapped around, his eyes flew down to her face. It might have been a trick of the dim lighting, but he could have sworn both her smile and the look in her eyes whispered, *I'm all yours.*

Oh, God. He was in *very* bad shape.

Determined to hold on to his resolve or die trying, he hustled her out of the car, into the house, and straight up to her bedroom door. All of a sudden putting some distance between them was critical.

"Brent?" Amazing, he thought a little desperately, the things a sex drive could read into a woman's voice.

"Yeah?"

"Thank you for taking me tonight. I had a good time."

"Well, uh, yeah. Sure. So did I. You'd better get some sleep now, honey. I'll see you in the morning." He stepped back.

"Brent?" She laid a hand on his arm, and his mouth went dry.

"What?" he croaked.

"Aren't you going to kiss me good night?"

Blood roared into his head. Sweating now, he wedged his fingers under the collar that had suddenly become two sizes too tight. "I don't . . . *ahem* . . . I don't think that's such a good idea," he choked out, and took another step in retreat.

"But—"

Jen bit her lower lip, and her gaze dropped to the floor. It hit him then that she *wanted* him to kiss her but was too shy to press the point. Didn't she understand that if he kissed her now, he wouldn't be able to stop there? Maybe she didn't. Maybe it was time to let her know just how close to the edge she'd shoved him.

"Jen." Praying his rapidly dwindling self-control

could withstand even the smallest, most innocuous bodily contact, he curled a finger under her chin and tilted up her face. That look, so miserably uncertain, sent tenderness washing through him. "Sweetheart, I'd like nothing more than to kiss you right now."

"Well, then—"

"But," he interjected, laying a finger over her lips, "if I do that, I'm going to want to do a whole lot more. Do you understand? I want you too much to stop at a kiss tonight."

She reached up, curled her fingers around his wrist, and tugged his hand away from her mouth. Swallowed and took a deep, trembling breath. Looking him right in the eye, she whispered, "Okay."

She understood. Trying to ignore the swift, sharp stab of disappointment, he smiled crookedly. "Go on in now. Tomorrow we'll—"

"No." She moistened her lips. "I mean, okay, we'll do a whole lot more."

His stomach went into immediate free fall. *He could not have heard what he thought he heard.* Shaking his head, he gaped down at her. "What?" he rasped. "What did you say?"

"I said . . ." With an unsteady little huff, she squared her shoulders. "I said we can do a whole lot more. Than kiss, I mean."

Catching her face between his palms, he stared at her. She might be blushing like the virgin she was, but her eyes told him she knew exactly what she was saying. Exactly what—and who—she wanted.

She meant it! She was going to let him make love with her! Tonight!

Dropping back his head, he groaned a heartfelt thanks. After planting a brief, hard kiss on that alluring mouth, he scooped her up and carried her toward his bedroom.

"Brent?" He heard excitement laced with just a touch of panic.

"It's all right, baby. I'll take care of you. We'll take it nice and slow, I promise."

He kicked the bedroom door closed with his heel and carried her over to a wing chair in front of the bank of windows. Before setting her down, he paused to look at her. Just look. He wanted to memorize this minute, and her face bathed in moonlight before he loved her for the first time.

Her first time. He'd have to go slow and easy. He only hoped he could.

Of course he already knew how he was going to go about it. After all, he'd had a long, sleepless night with nothing to do but plan. He wanted to love her right, make it good for her.

Lowering her into the chair, he crouched in front of her. Stroked a finger down her cheek. "Tonight," he murmured, "is for you." She opened her mouth, but he shook his head. "Just for you," he repeated, and standing, slipped off his jacket.

The way he said *just for you* sent her stomach into a roller-coaster-style dip. Jen swallowed. Oh, boy.

Wide-eyed, she watched him unknot his tie and toss it aside. The cummerbund went next so he could tug his shirttail out of his slacks. He sat down on the bed and took off his shoes and socks.

"Now," he said, rising and crossing to stand in front of her, "you leave everything to me. I won't hurt you, sweetheart, I swear. All you have to do is tell me what you like. Okay?"

She wasn't sure, but she thought she nodded. His long, tanned fingers went to the top stud on his shirt. He slid it free. *He was undressing.* Jen's long-deprived hormones heated, simmered, and boiled right over.

"We're going to be good together, honey. So good," he growled, and slipped another stud. "I'm already burning for you." His eyes closed on a deep breath, then opened. Trapped in that heated gaze, she felt the first lick of flames. "God, Jen, I have to touch you."

He stepped forward to trace a finger down her throat and across her collarbone, slipping it under the edge of her bodice, where he stroked it lazily back and forth. His touch was light, but her breasts swelled and her nipples shrank into aching buds. Dimly, she wondered if he could see her heart try to pound its way out of her chest.

"So soft," he whispered. "Like silk." Torturously, almost reluctantly, he inched his finger out of her bodice and moved away again, making short work of the remaining shirt studs.

Eyes glued to his busy hands, Jen tried to moisten her lips, but her mouth was dry.

New sensations sprinted through her. Anticipation almost paralyzed her lungs. She had to remind herself to breathe.

When the last stud on his shirt was undone, he planted his hands on the arms of the chair and bent forward, tantalizing her with a view of that spectacular chest. As if they had a mind of their own, her hands fluttered upward.

"Yes," he whispered, and their gazes locked. "Put your hands on me. Please."

Squatting, he captured her fingers in his and carried her hands to his chest, guiding them in slow circles. Warm, hard muscles and soft hair—the abrasion had her palms tingling. Her fingertips brushed a flat male nipple, and he hissed, pulling her hands away and trapping them against the arms of the chair, covering fingers that flexed yearningly.

He nuzzled the hair away from her face, leaning in to dip his tongue into her ear. "I know, baby, I know. But . . . it's too much right now." Breathed into her ear, the words sent chills chasing up her arms. He nipped her earlobe and another delicate shiver shimmied up from her toes. She couldn't help it, she groaned.

"What's the matter, honey?" he murmured against her throat. "Cold?"

She shook her head. Cold? Not even if she was packed in ice! The curve of his lips when they slid back to brush hers said he knew exactly how she felt.

He nipped at her bottom lip. "Kiss me, Jen."

He didn't have to ask twice; she was already closing the distance between them. As soon as their lips met, she opened her mouth, throwing everything she had into her kiss—love, desire, and aching frustration. She was darkly pleased to hear him groan and feel him shudder. He broke away, and backed up a step.

"You're a dangerous woman, Jen Casey," he admitted breathlessly, and reached for his zipper. Jen's nerves snapped to painful attention. *Now we're getting to the good stuff.* She noticed then that his hands were shaking. Well, fair was fair. She was shaking all over. "What you do to me is a crime."

What *she* did to *him?* Was he kidding, or what? Nothing she had in her power to do could possibly compare with what he was doing to her, making her ache and want until she was nothing but a fiery bundle of need. *She* was the one on the brink of a heart attack. His zipper rasped and he started to slide off his slacks and briefs. *Forget the heart attack*, she thought wildly, *I'll spontaneously combust long before that.*

Finally he stood facing her, giving her her first good look at him. All of him. The two or three molecules of oxygen left in her lungs evaporated.

He was absolutely perfect. Wide shoulders, brawny arms, and a broad, beautifully sculpted chest sprinkled with dark gold hair. His stomach was washboard flat, bisected by a line of hair that arrowed down to his . . .

Oh . . . my . . . God!

Brent Maddox was all man. And then some.

"I, ah . . ." She swallowed. "That is, I don't think we'll be able to . . ." Gripping the chair, she tried again. After all, this was an important point—one that had to be cleared up before they tried to go any further. "This isn't going to work at all," she moaned.

He chuckled warmly and tugged her up out of the chair. "Don't worry, love," he murmured, "we'll fit. All you have to do is want me."

"I do want you, Brent," she breathed. On that she was absolutely clear. Screwing up her courage, she pulled her hands out of his grasp and placed them on his chest. Encouraged by his deep purr of approval, she skimmed his pectorals, then explored the width of his shoulders. "God, you're gorgeous," just slipped out, but she couldn't be sorry.

"Ah, honey. You're so damned sweet." He gathered her against his big body. Surrounded by heat, excited by the erection pressing against her belly, she snaked her arms around his neck and raised her face for his kiss.

His mouth slanted over hers, hot and avid, his tongue plunging deep. The ache between her thighs built, throbbing almost unbearably as his hips moved against her. By the time he broke the kiss, they were both breathing in ragged gasps, and she was crazy for him. Hands fisted in his hair, she whimpered and tried to tug him back to her.

"God, baby, give me a second," he rasped, and tucked her head under his chin. "Just a second."

Locked against his heaving chest, she inhaled the mingled scents of cologne and man and muttered, "I don't think I have a second."

"Oh, sweetheart, you're wrong. We've got all night." Dropping a kiss on top of her head, he set her away from him. "And right now I want to see you." He reached behind her for the zipper of her dress.

All of a sudden she remembered the pictures—Brent with one stunning woman after another. Models, actresses, and debutantes paraded through her mind, mocking her. Jen's hands flew up to clutch the material against her breasts.

Brent laid his hands on her shoulders and cocked his head. "What is it, Jen? What's wrong?"

"Brent, I—" She broke off. How could she tell him she was afraid she wouldn't measure up? "All those other women . . . I'm not—"

"No," he murmured, grasping her wrists to gently pull her hands away. "You're not. You're Jen Casey, the woman I want more than I want my next breath.

Believe me, baby, the others are old news; they don't matter. Not anymore. Nobody will be in our bed but you and me."

She forced herself to stand quietly as he unzipped the dress and hooked his fingers in the bodice to peel it downward, kneeling at her feet as she stepped out of it. Sitting back on his haunches, he let his gaze travel slowly up her legs, which were still clad in black thigh-highs. It lingered on her black French-cut panties and matching strapless bra. By the time they reached her face, his eyes glowed blue hot.

"Jesus, woman, you look good enough to eat."

Jen stared down at him, her body all but vibrating in the aftermath of his visual caress. "I do?" she squeaked.

"Oh, yeah," he drawled. "Let me show you."

His hands slid up the backs of her legs, and vibration increased to outright trembling. His warm mouth touched her kneecap, dampening skin and silk. Rising up on his knees, he skimmed his palms higher to grasp her thighs, while his tongue traced the lace edge of one stocking. When he lapped at the other stocking, her knees gave out, and she had to brace her hands on his shoulders.

"Mmm. Delicious." He nibbled and licked his way over her panties to her abdomen. His hands cupped her breasts, fingers flexing rhythmically. Heat pulsed under his hands and rippled outward. Jen dropped back her head on a groan, and Brent surged to his feet, sweeping her into his arms.

Somehow they ended up on the bed with Brent braced on his forearms above her. Jen smoothed her hands up his chest and behind his neck. His eyes riveted her with a look that scorched every cell in her body, clear down to and including the ones in her toenails.

"Are you sure, Jen?" He moved against her.

Her whispered *yes* was lost under the onslaught of his lips. Still braced over her, he made sizzling love to her mouth, and he did it forever. The thrust and stroke of his tongue was raw sex, and it drove her wild.

She didn't realize he'd taken off her bra and panties until he lowered himself on top of her. His heat and hardness branded her from breast to thigh and brought her arching to meet him.

"Good," he murmured against her throat. "Oh, love, you feel so damned good. I've been going crazy thinking of us here, like this." His mouth took hers again.

Suddenly his hands were everywhere. Stroking, pressing, and squeezing. Her body came almost terrifyingly alive, every inch burning like a furnace. She ached and hungered and writhed under him. His mouth raced after his hands, fanning the flames while the pressure inside her built. And built.

He left her to take something out of the table next to the bed, and she moaned, clutching at him mindlessly.

"I know, honey. Believe me, I know." Then he was back. "Are you ready for me, Jen?" he asked, positioning himself above her. Another deep kiss while his fingers moved between her thighs, probing. "Yeah, yeah, you're ready."

Was she? She didn't know. She only knew she'd go out of her mind if he didn't do something. His fingers feathered over some mysterious spot between her legs, and she clenched unbearably. "Brent. I want . . . Something's—"

"Let it happen, baby. Come on, let it happen." His fingers moved again. It was agonizing. It was beautiful. It was all too much. Everything inside her contracted until she thought she would implode, like a rubber band winding tighter. Unbearably tight.

"Please," she whimpered.

Then one finger slipped inside her, and the tension, already stretched wire-taut, snapped. The world exploded into glittering fragments.

Brent withdrew his hand, surged inside her in one hard thrust, then stopped. She cried out.

"Are you all right, baby?" he gritted out. "Is the pain going away?"

Pain? What pain? All she could feel were fullness and ecstasy.

Brent groaned. "God. So tight. Wet. I have to—" Just as the crest started to subside he moved and drove her right back over the edge. This time, she brought him over with her.

Lazy, hazy minutes drifted by. Jen wasn't sure where he'd taken her, but while the trip out had been a rocket launch, the return was a long, languid glide.

Awareness seeped in, one sensation at a time. Satin against her back, slick but rumpled. The big, damp body sprawled heavily on top of her. Choppy breaths puffing against her neck.

As he slid off her and pulled her against him, she strung together the first two words she could come up with. "Holy Ike."

He chuckled. "Yeah."

Brent propped himself on one elbow and looked

down at her. Reaching out an index finger, he gently traced her kiss-swollen lips. "Are you all right?"

Still stunned, but a bit more cognizant, she nodded. "So *that's* what all the fuss is about."

His smile dawned slowly, tenderly, and was touched with a hint of male arrogance. He bobbed his eyebrows. "Pretty good, huh?"

Pretty good? The man was a master at understatement.

"Maybe," she allowed, and yawned.

He laughed softly. "Witch. Hold on, I'll be right back." She watched him go into the bathroom and return with a wet washcloth. Blushing furiously, she managed an under-the-covers cleanup and gave it back, shooting him a disgruntled, embarrassed glower before he padded away.

By the time he climbed back in beside her, she was half-asleep. Closing her eyes, she snuggled deeper into the curve of his body. He was so warm, and she was so tired. "It was probably good, but I'll have to try it again, just to be sure," she murmured, drifting.

"Anytime, sweetheart. Anytime." He tugged the comforter over them.

"What a great way to spend a vacation." She sighed. The last thing she felt was his arm slipping around her waist.

She'd fallen asleep with a smile on her face. That made one of them. Brent didn't think he'd get to sleep anytime soon.

With one arm wrapped around Jen and the other crooked behind his head, he stared out at the moonlit Pacific. If he thought long and hard and all night long, by morning he might come to grips with what had just happened to him.

Whatever the hell that was.

He knew about good sex. If two people got to know each other and liked one another pretty well, the sex was usually good. Fun. Enjoyable.

Great sex?

Great sex was harder to come by. It took more than two people liking each other. Great sex needed that spark, that almost uncontrollable physical attraction. Combine chemicals and compatibility, and you had all the makings of a first-class affair. Rowdy, sweaty sex. And often, if you were lucky.

Great sex was what he'd expected with Jen Casey. What he got was something more.

She'd given him everything. Not just her body— everything. And he, it seemed, had had no choice but to give it all right back to her. Only now he had a feeling he'd unwittingly given away pieces of himself he hadn't even known about. Important pieces, and ones he'd never get back.

That the earth had moved made sense if you looked at it objectively. With that level of total emotional involvement, physical sensation had been almost unbearably heightened. He'd felt as if he were absorbing her, being absorbed *by* her.

The scariest part was that he still felt a connection, the satisfaction that was more than physical. Could two people really be joined that deeply? Evidently. But it was something new in his experience, and it worried the hell out of him.

Maybe it would go away. He sure hoped so.

Brent didn't like feeling as if his body had made some kind of commitment without his brain's permission. Would he still feel this way in the morning? And if he did, what was he going to do about it?

Questions. He had lots of questions.

Jen stirred in her sleep. Unconsciously, he tightened his hold on her. Yeah, he had questions, and the longer he was around her, the more questions he seemed to come up with. What he didn't have, yet, were answers.

And he only had a few days to get them.

TEN

The struggle for understanding had been uphill and futile, leaving him next door to brain-dead at the tail end of another sleepless night. Raking a weary hand through his hair, Brent cursed the churning thoughts that had driven him out of a warm bed and away from an even warmer woman to stalk the beach and stew away the hours before dawn.

He tossed back his Scotch and spared a wry glance at the perfect rosebud dangling from the fingers of his left hand. Stalking and stewing were bad enough, but he'd plucked the bud from the bank of wild roses tumbling along the path to the house because the blooms were soft, vibrant and sweet-smelling, and reminded him of Jen. Well, hell. Before he knew it, he remembered that bit about some guy's love being "like a red, red rose."

A man was in bad shape when he brooded over a woman and thought of lines from Robert Burns.

Standing on the patio watching dawn limn the fringe of palms along the beach, Brent rocked back on

his heels and wondered whether to be amused,
amazed, or annoyed by his pitiful condition. All of the
above, he finally decided with a sardonic twist of his
lips.

There was only one explanation. "She's making
me crazy."

Dropping back his head, he squinted into the
brightening sky. His time for soul-searching had run
out. Pretty soon Crampton would send the staff
scrambling, and the commotion would wake up Jen.
Women were funny about finding themselves in bed
alone on first mornings after, so he'd be there when
she opened her eyes. He might not know what to
make of her, but he wouldn't hurt her when it could
be so easily avoided.

Heaving a tired sigh, he turned and slipped
through the sliding glass doors. He was halfway
across the dining room when Crampton barked,
"What do you think you're doing?" and scared him
out of ten years' growth.

Stumbling back, he regained his balance just short
of toppling through the door, butt first. He glowered
at his housekeeper. "Dammit, woman, you scared the
hell out of me!"

"Hmm." Lips pursed, Crampton crossed her arms
and looked down. Brent followed her gaze. Salt water
dripped daintily off the cuffs of his gray linen slacks,
dribbling tiny puddles through the sand drizzled
across the limestone floor.

Squelching a guilty squirm, he reluctantly met her
glare. Forced himself to hike up his chin and remember who was boss. "I went for a walk."

Crampton's fingers did a silent drumroll across a

left bicep Stallone would envy. One iron-gray eye-brow arched derisively. "A walk in the ocean."

"Yeah." His shoulders shifted self-consciously, be-cause it sounded stupid. "Partly."

Snake-quick, the housekeeper reached out to snatch the glass from his hand. She lifted it to her nose, sniffed, and snorted disdainfully. "Drunk."

"I am not! I had one drink," he mumbled. "Just one."

"Is that right?"

"That's right." Squaring his shoulders, he ordered himself to stop with the hand-in-the-cookie-jar expla-nations and act like the one in charge. He started forward. "Now, if you'll excuse me, I'll just go—"

A work-roughened hand slapped against his black T-shirt. "Hold it." Althea's gaze dropped to his sandy feet, and the hand on his chest shoved. "Out."

Caught off guard, Brent could do no more than blink as he shuffled backward. "Out? No, I—" But she'd already bulldozed him onto the patio. "Wait a minute—"

"*You* wait. Right here." Crampton dropped her hand and pinned him with a narrow, or-else stare. "I'll be back," she warned.

"Thinks she's Schwarzenegger," he mumbled, but not until she was out of earshot. Dropping to sit side-ways on the nearest chaise, he gave a disgruntled huff. "Women."

Banished from his own house with nobody but himself for company, it wasn't long before his thoughts scurried into the same maze they'd wan-dered for hours, squirreling in circles as he tried to figure out Jen and what she'd done to him.

He closed his eyes, remembering the sense of having given up something vital. A fragment of his . . . what? His heart? He ran a hand over his chest as if to make sure the organ was still there.

Or maybe he'd relinquished a scrap of his soul.

The possibility scared him into thinking out loud. "She doesn't hold anything back, dammit, just gives you everything. And before you know it, you're giving right back to her." He cursed. "Even if you don't want to."

Fired up, he rose to pace. "Then, when it's all over and too late to protect yourself, you realize you've given her things you can't take back. You feel like you've made some kind of commitment, only you didn't mean to."

"Got you talking to yourself, has she?"

Confused, Brent answered without thinking. "Yeah."

Then it hit him. Crampton had asked him a question! His head snapped around, and he gaped at the imposing bulk filling the doorway. A *personal* question.

"About time you found a good woman and settled down," she announced with a curt nod, and fired at towel at his head.

He snagged the towel in self-defense as his jaw dropped. "Settle down? What in the hell are you talking about? I'm not ready to settle down! Christ, I barely know the woman!"

Althea grumbled something about knee-jerk reactions and bachelors right before she planted her hands on her hips and snapped, "Don't know her? You sure about that?"

Rubbing at the knots in the back of his neck, Brent grappled with the realization that he and

Crampton Bligh were having an actual conversation—with sentences and everything. "What do you mean?"

Crampton rolled her eyes and pointed at the chaise. "Clean off your feet."

"I don't know her," he insisted, but sat and brushed halfheartedly at his feet, suddenly thoughtful. "Well, not really. Of course, we did go to high school together."

"Well, then."

"She's honest," he continued absently. "Plucky too." His lips curved. "Enjoys the hell out of life. Got more than her share of common sense, half her share of coordination, and honesty and integrity that run bone-deep."

"She's crazy about you."

Brent's gaze snapped to Althea's face. "Crazy about me?"

"She loves you."

He shook his head as if to clear it. Lack of sleep must have dulled his brain. "Loves me?"

Crampton shook her head. "Thick as a brick," she muttered, and marched off, leaving Brent to stare after her.

The undeniable bolt of truth stunned him. Zapped him like thirty thousand volts, damned near knocked him off his chaise, and left him reeling.

Jen loved him.

Simple, really, and if he hadn't been so desperate for her, he would've picked up on it the minute the words *we can do a whole lot more than kiss* left her mouth. A woman like Jen didn't have sex with a man unless she loved him.

Love was the unknown that shot them straight

past great sex into what he belatedly recognized as making love.

And making love implied commitment.

Conflicting emotions blossomed in his chest, panic and denial leading the pack. He wanted to cut and run. He didn't want to know she loved him, and knowing, didn't want to go back and face her.

But bubbling alongside the panic was giddy amazement and, as insane as it sounded, satisfaction. Every bit as much as he wanted to run, he wanted to go back and wrap his arms around her, kiss her awake, and seduce her into admitting her feelings out loud. He needed to hear the words.

"I'm cracking up," he decided, and swiped determinedly at his feet.

She loved him, he thought again, and his hand slowed. For the man he was, not his money or his looks or his notoriety. He knew it with a certainty that rocked him to his restless soul.

It was humbling.

It was exciting.

It was terrifying.

"You still out here?"

Brent's turbulent blue gaze lifted to the over-starched woman striding toward him. "She loves me. What in God's name am I going to do now?"

Althea stopped dead. "You asking me?"

It didn't make any sense but, "Yeah."

For the first time since he'd known her, Crampton looked uncomfortable. "Why?"

"Damned if I know." He rubbed his temple and pictured Jen. "I can't get a handle on this."

The housekeeper's eyebrows puckered into what

he guessed was a thoughtful frown. "Well . . . How do you feel about her?"

"How do I feel about her?" He knew what it felt like to be deep inside her. He knew the physical act had been intense enough to sear through to the emotional level; it had forged a bond that lingered even when their bodies were no longer joined. But did he love her? "I haven't got a clue."

Althea gifted him with a pitying look. "Typical."

Great. The Terminator felt sorry for him. Brent shot her an impatient glance. "So where do I go from here?"

"Where do you want to go?"

"Well, half of me wants to back off."

"Gutless."

Brent grimaced. "You got it."

That cowardly half wanted to go back a few hours, forget the introspection, and drop directly off to sleep. Then, still blissfully ignorant, he'd drift awake and slip into Jen before drowsiness cleared away. They'd spend the next few days talking and laughing and making love, then he'd let her go and get on with his new, improved life, heart-whole.

Crampton looked oddly disappointed. "Guess you could do that."

Brent smiled ruefully. "Nope. Too late. I'm in too deep." He dragged a hand down his face and sighed. "She's got something, Althea. I don't know what it is, but I need it." He wanted to grab onto the possibilities Jen's love offered and find out where and how far they would take him. But . . . "She never said the words, you know."

Did that mean she'd tuck her love into some protected corner of her heart and walk out of his life a few days from now? The fear that she might do exactly that spawned a curl in his gut. "She might leave."

"Don't let her."

"How am I supposed to stop her?"

Crampton snorted. "Sweet talk."

"Oh. Uh . . . yeah." But somehow, he couldn't imagine feeding Jen the usual lines. Of course, she'd probably stay if he said he loved her, but he'd never said those words to a woman before. How could he say them now, when he didn't know whether or not they were true?

"She doesn't think much of my lifestyle," he admitted glumly.

"She'll come around."

"Uh-huh." Brent smiled thinly. "Know what she said?"

"What?"

"She said, 'What a great way to spend a vacation.'" His fingers clamped a stranglehold on the towel. "And I wanted to say, 'That's no vacation, that's my life.'"

Evidently at a loss for an answer, Althea settled for "Hmm," grabbed the towel, and stalked into the house. Caught up in yet another bout of unwelcome realization, Brent barely noticed her departure.

Damn! Until Jen waltzed back into his life, he'd thought it was a pretty good one. The first glimmer to the contrary had dawned in the face of her burning enthusiasm for her job. He'd suffered vague twitches of discontent on and off ever since, but sometime during the night, discontent had crystallized into disillusionment and dissatisfaction.

He stood and wandered over to lean on the low

brick wall. "You know," he mused wistfully, and to no one in particular, "up until a few weeks ago I liked my life. It's fast-paced. Active." He sighed. "And boring, dammit. Except back then it didn't bother me so much." So this was enlightenment. "Who needs it?"

Needed or not, wanted or not, the revelations kept coming.

His best friends, like Mitch, had responsibilities tied to their money. Was that why he preferred their company to that of the idle rich, like himself? Had he always envied Mitch the sense of purpose that went hand in hand with his duties as CEO?

Suddenly Brent wondered if one of the things that attracted him about serving on the boards of various charities wasn't the fact that they gave him direction and the feeling of a job well done. That would certainly explain why he'd done more and more of that kind of work in recent years.

But would it be enough? Or would he drift through the future the way he'd drifted through the last twelve years?

Swearing impatiently, he pushed away from the wall and strode into the house. Christ, he was a mess! A wonderful, sexy-cute woman was in love with him, and he—sorry, mixed-up bastard that he was—couldn't even figure out whether or not he felt the same about her.

Crampton all but plowed into him as he rounded a corner. "What now?"

Seething with frustration, Brent tossed up a hand. "You tell me! Suppose I did love her? What then?"

"Then there's no problem." With a shake of her head, Althea pushed past him.

No problem? Of course there would be problems,

Brent thought as he climbed the stairs. Jen had a meaningful career, one that she loved. How would she relate to a man who had no career at all? A man who served no useful purpose? Ten years from now, would she—and everybody else, for that matter—look at him and see nothing more than an aging playboy?

Imagining it, he ground his teeth. God, but that would scrape his pride! And he'd have no defense, because he'd be every bit the useless appendage they took him for. Knowing it would twist him into a bitter man without an ounce of self-respect, one who wouldn't have it in him to make himself or anybody else happy.

Jen Casey deserved better than that.

He paused at the bedroom door to gaze at the small, curvy bundle of rumpled green satin and soft woman curled in the middle of his bed. Shaking his head, he closed the door behind him and crossed the room.

She slept on her back, one arm outflung, palm up and fingers curled. Her hair spread like a tangled, glossy brown halo across the pillow. Those full, rosy lips were parted slightly, as if begging for his kiss. One deep pink nipple peeked out over the top edge of the comforter, one small foot out the bottom. She still had her stockings on—he'd never gotten around to skinning them off those trim legs.

Desire rammed him squarely in the gut, leaving him breathless. Desire and aching tenderness. Dammit, how did she do this to him? How could she look sexy and adorable, all at the same time? He was as hard as Crampton's precious limestone floor, and Jen wasn't even awake yet.

He hesitated only briefly. His lips quirked. Tossing the rose over his shoulder, he stripped off his shirt, pants, and briefs then knelt on the bed. She wasn't awake yet, but she *would* be in just a minute.

"Jen." Bracing a hand on either side of her head, he leaned down to kiss each eyelid softly. "Jennifer. Come on, baby, wake up."

"*Hmmm?*" Her mouth curved dreamily. Languorously, she stretched like a contented little tabby. The slow, sleepy undulation brushed her body up against his, a sensation so sweet and sensual, he couldn't help but growl with pleasure.

"Come on, sweetheart," he murmured huskily, "open your eyes."

As his mouth settled over hers he skimmed a hand down her body, sweeping away the sheets and comforter. Her lips opened to his seeking tongue just as his fingers closed over a creamy breast, and he captured her gasp. Rolling her nipple between thumb and forefinger, he took the kiss deeper. He nipped at her lower lip before nibbling his way across her cheek and down her neck. The skin against his lips was warm, flushed with sleep and rapidly budding arousal.

"Are you awake yet?" he whispered.

"Oh, yes," she breathed, twining her arms around his neck. Her silk-covered foot skimmed up his calf. "Yes, I'm definitely awake." But she didn't open her eyes.

Releasing her breast, he let his hand glide down to her stomach. Then lower. "Are you sure?" In spite of his own fierce need, he smiled when she tossed her head and moaned. "Is that a yes?"

"Brent . . ." Beneath him, she shifted restively. His fingers wriggled tauntingly and her hips arched toward him. "I just want to make sure, honey. I wouldn't want you to miss anything."

At that her eyelids fluttered open to reveal eyes fathomless and misty with passion, the brown almost eclipsed by the iris. "I already told you, I'm—"

He closed her mouth with a drugging kiss—at least, it damned well drugged him. It had to be her taste—hot, wild honey laced with white lightning, one hundred eighty proof. It went right to his head every time. Desire pounded through him, sending his mouth down her body. He swept off her stockings, one at a time, dragging his lips and tongue down after them.

Jen went wild. "Brent! Brent, you come back here!"

After a quick pause for protection, he surged back up, settling between her legs, cutting off her demands with another devouring kiss. "Are you sore?" He was on fire. He didn't know what he'd do if she said yes.

Her hips lifted, searching. "What?" she gasped.

"Sore." He eased one finger inside her. So tight. Wet. God, so hot. "Are you sore?"

"Oooooh," she crooned. Then: "No, no, I'm not sore."

"Good." He positioned himself, probing. Linking his hands with hers, he thrust slow and sure. The slick, tight clasp of her body almost pulled him straight into climax. Gritting his teeth, he fought the urge to come. Not yet. Not yet.

"Brent." She lifted herself into his next thrust. "Oh, Brent . . . You feel so good."

The breathless words, combined with the slow, grinding gyration of her hips as she fought for release dragged him closer to the edge. He let go of her hands to brace himself over her. Watched as he drove into her. Again. And again. "Come, baby. Please come. I can't wait."

"Yes. Oh, Brent, *yesss.*"

Her hands flew up to grip his shoulders, and he knew he'd be marked. The last thin thread on his control snapped clean, and he plunged wildly as Jen's legs wound around him, drawing him deeper.

"Brent! Oh my God, Brent!"

"Brent?"

"What?" he mumbled against her shoulder.

"There's a rose on the floor." She could just glimpse it at the edge of her vision, a tight red bud punctuating the cream expanse of the carpet.

She wouldn't have noticed it at all if her head hadn't been hanging over the side of the bed. A few minutes from now when she recovered the remnants of her scattered wits, she'd try to figure out how she ended up in this position. Jen wriggled herself back onto the mattress.

" 'S for you." Brent shifted. Now he was lying half on top of her. It might have been his hard parts sliding across her soft parts, or the air hitting her damp body, but she shivered. He must have felt it, because he grunted and reached back to tug a corner of the comforter over them.

But Jen's attention was all for the rose. "For me?" Entranced, she felt her lips curve into a slow smile. "You picked me a rose?"

"Mmm."

"Thank you."

"Mmm."

Evidently, the rose wouldn't be accompanied by any flowery speeches or declarations. Unless she missed her guess, she thought tenderly, reaching up to stroke his hair, her lover would shortly be sound asleep.

Her lover. She still couldn't quite believe she had one. It was even harder to believe that the lover was Brent. He could have had any woman he wanted, but he'd wanted her—Jennifer Marie Casey, small-town schoolteacher and ex-president of the Donnerton High Poetry Club. It was nothing short of mind-boggling.

Almost as mind-boggling as the things she'd learned about herself during the last twelve hours. Who would've thought she'd be so . . . *wild and passionate?* she decided with a blush. Good Lord, once those hormones of hers got together with the right catalyst, namely one sexy tower of golden manpower called Brent Maddox, they were positively explosive! Looking back, her wild response to his every touch astounded her.

All things considered, she felt pretty darned proud of herself.

Wouldn't Candy be surprised to find out her best friend was a wanton at heart? A woman who indulged in stormy lovemaking and ended up with her head hanging off the side of the bed? *Pure as the driven snow, my foot,* Jen thought, gloating silently. She only wished she had the nerve to *tell* Candy.

Judging from the gentle snores, Brent was dead to the world. Jen would have been happy to lie half under him all day, but contrary to what she'd told him in the heat of the needy moment, she *was* just a little sore. Somewhere in this big old house there was a hot bath with her name on it. Trying not to wake him, she edged out from under his body and slid off the bed.

She looked down at him, and her heart ballooned almost painfully, pressing tears into her eyes. Dear God, but she loved that man. Loved him so much, she hurt inside. *Please, please let him feel the same.*

She sniffed back the silly tears and straightened her shoulders. If she didn't get out of here fast, she was going to cry all over him. And how would she explain it when he woke up drenched in saline?

His closet was almost as big as her bedroom at home, but she managed to locate a thick navy-blue robe among all the Armani, Versace, and Gucci. Slipping it on and drawing the plush terry cloth around her, she tiptoed across the carpet into the spacious master bath.

"Oh God, would you look at that?"

A gleaming black marble bathtub had been sunk in front of the glass wall, which evidently extended into this room from the bedroom. A closer inspection of the tub revealed whirlpool jets. Jen figured this was as close to heaven as a bathroom could get and turned on the taps.

There was something deliciously decadent about being naked in front of the entire Pacific Ocean, she mused a few minutes later, sinking into the swirling waters with an ecstatic sigh. The water reached her shoulders and was hot enough to waft steam into her face. This was something else she'd gladly do all day long, especially if Brent climbed in with her.

That errant thought started a chain reaction, calling up a series of ideas so erotic Jen wondered if she wouldn't have been better off filling the tub with *cold* water. Where *had* this bawdy turn of mind come from? "And how do I turn it off before the bathwater boils?"

Leaning her head back against the rim of the bathtub, she closed her eyes and dragged her thoughts to a higher plane. Making love with Brent signaled a major change in her life. It was time to think about what that change meant and what might, or might not, happen because of it.

In a perfect world, Brent would be sensitive enough to guess that she'd *made* love with him because she was *in* love with him. In that world, he would be touched, maybe even overjoyed. Definitely overjoyed. He'd love her, too, and ask her to marry him so they could live happily ever after.

Unfortunately, this was not a perfect world. She picked up a cake of soap and leisurely lathered her arms. The soap smelled like Brent. Determined not to get sidetracked by scent association, but to face reality, no matter how unpleasant, head-on, she rubbed more vigorously, as if friction alone could bring her back to the subject at hand.

Thankfully, she was now an ex-snob, or well on her way to becoming one. But just because she'd decided their contrasting lifestyles weren't a problem didn't mean Brent would see things that way. He said he needed her, seemed to care about her, certainly seemed to enjoy making love to her, but those things didn't mean she was the kind of woman he wanted to spend his life with.

If he was ready to settle down at all.

If he was, he might be looking for something else entirely in a wife. The newly love-tender heart in her breast shuddered at the thought. Setting her jaw, Jen shoved the soap across her shoulder.

He might want a woman who'd fit seamlessly into his life and world. "A *sophisticated* woman who wouldn't gawk like a hayseed just because she comes face-to-face with a limousine. The big dope."

Thoroughly incensed, she dunked her sudsy arms and shoulders.

And what about her career? She loved teaching. How would Brent feel about his wife working? Did he work? If not, would he expect her to give up teaching and become a high-living world traveler along with him? Or a glittering socialite?

Scowling ferociously, she snatched up the soap again. She loved him and was more than willing to compromise on a lot of things, but not that. If she gave up her career she'd be miserable, and make him miserable right along with her.

She plopped her right leg on the edge of the tub and attacked it with the soap. Counting today, they had four days left of their week together. Would those four days give them enough time to settle things between them?

Granted, they'd known each other for years, but that had been a long, long time ago. The relationship they had now was a whole new ball game. How in the heck was it supposed to turn into a lasting commitment if they were only together for a few more days? The least he could do was ask her to stay longer.

"Honestly, men can be such blockheads!"

Plunging her right leg back into the water, she jerked out the left one. She'd happily agree to stay longer if he asked. And what if he didn't? Was she supposed to crawl meekly back to Donnerton and forget she'd ever seen him? Pretend she'd never lain with him and felt him moving inside her? Her left leg hit the water with a solid splash.

"Not in this lifetime, brother."

Her chin jutted out as she slapped down the soap. She could and would fight for him. No, for them. Making love had been a darned good start, but she wanted more than a physical relationship from him. If that meant laying her cards faceup on the table, so be it. She'd tell him how she felt about him, all right. The prospect was daunting enough to tie her stomach in a knot, but daunting wasn't going to stop her.

Sometime before their time was up, she was going to sit Brent Maddox down, pin him eyeball to eyeball, and tell him straight out that she was crazy in love with him, and what was he going to do about it?

Fired with righteous resolve, she shot to her feet. Water sluiced down her body as she stepped out of the tub, whipping a thick white bath sheet off the heated towel bar. Yes sir, she would lay her heart smack dab on the line, right there at his feet.

"If he doesn't have sense enough to pick it up . . . well, I'll just have to get tough."

This was one fight she didn't intend to lose.

ELEVEN

"Jen, this is Bill Williamson. Bill, Jennifer Casey."

"Hello, Mr. Williamson." Hoping her smile was relaxed enough to camouflage her jumping nerves, Jen offered her hand. The portly Williamson grabbed it and pumped enthusiastically.

"Just make that Bill, little lady," he drawled. "Pleased to meet you." His accent was chaps and Stetson, his suit charcoal silk with pinstripes.

"Bill is chairman of the board for United Charities. Their national headquarters is in Dallas, but he was kind enough to give up his Sunday and fly in for a look at our setup. We're trying to get United's backing for Hope Away from Home."

Translation: This meeting was important. Okay. Pep talk.

Don't do anything stupid, Jennifer. Stay calm. Poised. Think quiet dignity and underlying supportiveness. You want Brent to be proud of you. This is your chance to show him how well you can move in his circles.

She'd known she had a foot in the door to Brent's

life the minute he asked her to come along with him this morning. Now all she had to do was keep it there without getting her toes smashed. The sooner she showed him how well she could fit in, the sooner he'd ask her to stay with him. She hoped.

Williamson took a long look around. "You've done some good work here, son. This is damned impressive."

This was a sprawling two-story house in San Clemente. White with blue trim. Flowers spilled a riot of color at the foot of the porch, bleeding rainbow hues over the lip of the broad lawn. A white picket fence marched brightly around the perimeter.

"The place needed quite a face-lift." Brent swung open the gate and waved them through. "We painted, added the handicapped-accessible ramps, modified the width of the doorways. The workmen left just last week."

The house exuded welcome, cheer, and . . . hope. It *was* impressive, Brent should be proud of himself. She was certainly proud of him.

Williamson nodded. "Like I said, damned impressive."

Brent tucked his hands into his pockets and shrugged. He looked a little proud and a lot self-conscious. Not to mention utterly delicious. Lord, what a dark blue suit did for those eyes. . . .

"Thanks," he was saying brusquely, "but I can't take much credit. We've got some good people working for the foundation, and we've been lucky as far as drumming up support."

"Hmm." Williamson glanced sideways at Brent. For a split second someone extremely shrewd peeked out of his broad, good-natured face. Someone who didn't buy Brent's personal disclaimer. Then the good old boy grinned back. The whole thing happened so fast, Jen blinked.

"Well, come on, then." Bill gestured expansively. "Are you gonna show me the whole shebang, or are we just gonna stand out here jawin' all day?"

Brent smiled slightly and started up the walk. "Right this way for the nickel tour."

"Real nice location, Maddox." Williamson stood on the porch and gazed across the lawn to the sedate, tree-lined neighborhood. "But how d'you reckon your folks'll get down to the medical center? USC, isn't it? If I remember right, that's a right far piece from here."

"A ways," Brent conceded as he unlocked the door. "But we didn't want to afflict our guests with downtown L.A. We'll have a couple of shuttles available for transport, day and night, and there's a heliport less than five miles from here we can use in emergencies."

"Smart thinkin'. Don't care much for town life myself—my spread's a few miles outside of Dallas, you know. Sure don't know how those folks in the city can stand it. Packed together like sardines in a can. Air's brown," he muttered, looking around the foyer. "Can't stand brown air."

Oh, boy. Foghorn Legghorn. Jen pressed her lips together. If Bill Williamson was going to talk like a cartoon chicken, she was a goner. Her bid for dignified composure would blow sky-high.

In an effort to distract herself, she focused on the entrance hall, and caught her breath. "Brent, this is beautiful." Swept away with excitement, she forgot to act the subdued, sophisticated companion. "I love hardwood floors! They make everything look so warm. Oh my gosh, is that an elevator?"

He smiled indulgently and reached out to take her hand. "Yeah. Come on, I'll take you through."

"Sort of makes you just want to come on in and sit a spell, don't it?" murmured Bill when they stepped into the living room.

That it did. The furniture was quality and obviously chosen with comfort and durability in mind. Most of the pieces were big, overstuffed, and earthtoned. Toys for all ages were jumbled in a huge built-in toy box. The big-screen television was rigged with a video-game system.

But it was the little touches that made the house something special. The rockers in every bedroom. And the fact that two bedrooms were equipped with cribs. Brent explained that the unfurnished room at the far end of the upstairs hall was reserved for a housekeeper.

The kitchen occupied the entire back half of the first floor. It was cheery and sun-filled and dominated by a huge oak table that would easily seat twenty.

"Hope Away from Home," Jen murmured. "It fits. There's so much love here. Already there's love, and it will touch every single person who walks through the door."

Brent had created this. Not by himself certainly, but it was his idea, his project. Somehow she knew that his enthusiasm, his caring were the foundations on which this lovely house had been built. The magnitude of his compassion and dedication struck her like a blow. Forgetting they weren't alone, forgetting her carefully thought-out plan of attack, forgetting everything but how incredibly wonderful he was, she flung herself into his unsuspecting arms.

"I'm so proud of you." She squeezed her eyes shut to contain the tears that welled, and buried her face against his chest.

His arms crept around her hesitantly. She lifted her head to look at his face. His expression was a curious mixture of stunned disbelief and tentative hope. "You're proud of me?"

Uh-oh. It was that please-tell-me-I'm-not-a-total-loser look. She'd seen it before, of course, written on the faces of some of her students. That sad, hopeful look never failed to move her to tears.

Seeing it on Brent's face almost brought her to her knees.

Jen tried to blink back the rising flood. Big, bad, beautiful Brent Maddox, playboy zillionaire and man of the world, needed to know somebody was proud of him. It seemed she had something he needed after all, but she'd think about that later. Right now she had a job to do.

"Of course I'm proud of you," she whispered fiercely. A rogue tear escaped to trickle down her cheek. "Very, very proud."

He caught the droplet on his fingertip, stared at it, then lifted his gaze to hers. His smile bloomed slowly, starting at slight, blossoming to broad and blinding. The finished product was enough to make a woman go weak in the knees. Thank goodness he was holding on to her.

"You're proud of me." This time he sounded as if he believed it.

He was going to kiss her, and heaven only knew, she needed to kiss him. He started to lower his head, she rose on tiptoe to meet him halfway. The voice that intruded from behind her had them leaping guiltily apart.

"Well now, isn't that nice?" Bill Williamson beamed like a proud papa. "Yes sir, that's real nice. And she's right, young fella. You've done a jam-up job here." He cleared his throat. "Now, where'd you say those other units will be located?"

Brent shot her a look of heated promise. That was unfortunate, because it reminded her of the delectable hours they had whiled away the night before last. In the hot tub.

And yesterday afternoon. On his sailboat.

Not to mention a couple of torrid hours last night. In his bed.

She was a ragged heartbeat away from dragging him upstairs to initiate one of the empty bedrooms when he turned to answer Bill's question. Good move, Jen thought, running a shaky hand over her hair. Not only had he managed to save his body and his virtue, he'd also robbed her of the perfect opportunity to make a complete fool of herself. *Get a grip, Jennifer!*

"We're already renovating a house just outside Philadelphia for people who need access to St. Jude's and the Wills Eye Hospital. We picked up a property near Rochester to cover the Mayo Clinic, and I'm negotiating for a place on the outskirts of Baltimore, which takes care of Johns Hopkins."

"What about staff?"

"Most of the positions are already filled. Each house will have its own live-in housekeeper, and a nurse-practitioner and counselor available on call."

Williamson tucked his thumbs into his vest pockets, dipped his chin once, and rocked back on his heels. "Sounds like you got everything worked out."

"We're doing our best." Brent led the way out into the backyard, which sported both a sandbox and a swing set. "So what do you think, Bill? Can we count on support from United?"

Once again, Williamson's friendly gaze honed to razor sharpness. Saying nothing, he reached into his inside coat pocket and drew out a cigar. It was about half a foot long and almost that big around, bilious green and ugly. When he lit up, Jen was forced concede the impossible. The cigar smelled worse than it looked.

"Might," he acknowledged finally. "We might could do that. What all you got in mind?"

Judging by the look in Brent's eye, he knew exactly what kind of man he was dealing with. "Some financial support, of course."

Eyes narrowed, Williamson nodded slowly. " 'Course."

"Public relations. United's PR department has an established track record, one of the best anywhere. Hope is the new kid on the block, charity-wise. We've been concentrating on logistics, just trying to get the houses fixed up, staffed, and ready to go into operation. We haven't had the time, money, or personnel to mount any comprehensive publicity effort. Without an effective PR campaign, we can't inform the public of our existence or the services we have available. We won't be able to raise the funds we'll need to keep paying the bills, either. If we're under the umbrella of United Charities, PR won't be a problem."

The ensuing silence was filled with birdsong and the combined scents of summer flowers and toxic cigar smoke. When the wait had stretched nearly to Jen's breaking point, Bill nodded.

"I'll bring it up at the next board meeting. They most always listen to my suggestions, and I've got to tell you, I don't think we'll run into any problems on this one."

Brent's quietly expelled breath was his only indication that the answer had been important to him. "Great." He smiled and clapped the other man lightly on the back. "I'll get the paperwork drawn up."

"And I'll get the ball rolling on my end. Now, there was one more thing I wanted to talk to you about, and I guess this is about as good a time as any. See, what I have in mind—"

"Mr. Williamson." A tall, thin man jogged around the side of the house. The black hair slicked straight back from his forehead was almost as shiny as his wing tips. "Mr. Williamson, you've got an urgent call on the car phone."

"Now, Clancy? Can't it wait?"

Tightening his already ruthlessly knotted tie, the messenger swallowed heavily. His dark eyes darted nervously from person to person. "N-no, sir," he stammered. "It's Dallas about the Day of Service Campaign funding. There's a glitch."

"Glitch? What kind of glitch?" But Williamson was already striding away, his stocky legs eating up terrain with surprising speed. Clancy scurried to catch up. "Damn bureaucrats, got no more sense than a bunch of hard-boiled eggs. Maddox, you wait right there. I'm not done with you." The order was rapped out as he disappeared around the corner.

"Yes, sir," Brent murmured sardonically. "Whatever you say, sir."

Suddenly he let out a joyous whoop, grabbed Jen, and swung her in a dizzying circle. "Hot damn, we did it!"

With a surprised shriek, Jen wrapped her arms around his neck and hung on. "Not we, you!" she laughed breathlessly. "You did it! You were great! Stupendous!"

Their pirouette slowed, but the lambent gleam in his eyes kept her head whirling even after their bodies had stopped. "And this means what? You're proud of me again?" he asked huskily.

Unable to tear her eyes away from his, she nodded. "Yes."

"How proud?"

"Bust-my-buttons proud."

His gaze dropped to her blouse. His lips curved wickedly. "Yeah?"

The heartbeat behind the buttons in question took off at a gallop. "Yeah."

"Sounds promising," he growled softly. Then, shaking his head, he sighed. "Later, baby. That guy, Clancy, would have a heart attack." His eyes crawled back up to her mouth, and he did a pitiful imitation of a wistful glance. "I might be able to hold off . . . if I had a little something to tide me over."

Jen could actually *feel* her lips heat and soften. And tingle. *Ho-ly Ike!* He really ought to register that stare. It was deadly.

"I've got just the thing," she whispered, and pulling down his head, kissed him.

She loved his mouth. She wanted to devour his mouth. But she wanted to make him wild first.

Changing the angle, she rubbed her lips lightly back and forth. Teasing. Tantalizing. Testing his control. She traced his mouth with her tongue, darting it away when he opened to her, enticing him to follow.

This was the first time *she* had kissed *him*. Excitement charged through her veins as she took them both deeper. Stroked, plunged, retreated, and seduced him with her mouth alone. When he groaned, clamping his arms even tighter and hauling her up against his muscled, aroused body, the thrill struck her like a lightning bolt.

This, then, was a woman's power.

She liked it.

She was just getting the hang of it, had in fact made him shudder and moan by biting down gently on his lower lip, when *that* voice drawled out behind them, "There y'all go again. I swear, you two are hotter than a couple of sheep in a pepper patch."

This unwelcome interruption dragged out a pair of quiet groans, which were not prompted by passion, but by dismay and exasperation. Jen pulled away and tried to tuck in her yellow linen blouse. *Somebody* had pulled it out of her matching skirt.

Before she could get herself completely undisheveled, Brent snatched her close, pressing her face against his chest. The jackhammer beat of his heart under her ear prompted a sly, secret smile.

"Just celebrating," he offered nonchalantly. Except he sounded as if he'd just run the four-minute mile. In two minutes.

Jen's smile widened. *She* had done that to him, winded him with nothing more than a kiss. Okay, so her heart and lungs were laboring just as badly. That wasn't important. What was important was the fact that *she* was responsible for getting them both in this embarrassing condition.

"That a fact?" Williamson chuckled. "Did some of that kind of celebrating myself in my day. Why, I remember once, there was this little gal down to—"

Oh, for goodness' sake. In another minute they'd be telling the kinds of stories indigenous to boys' locker rooms. Quickly ducking out from under Brent's arms, Jen turned to toss out a surefire diversion.

"Did you get your glitch straightened out, Bill?"

Bull's-eye. Bill scowled and yanked the cigar out of his mouth. "Hell no. Some big, high mucketymuck from New York City got himself all hot under the collar. Seems he decided to pay us a surprise visit and I wasn't there to lead him around by the nose." He swore, then looked apologetic. "Like I should jump when he says frog, and on a Sunday too. Now I got to fly back down to Dallas and soothe his ruffled feathers before he craps out on us. Politics." He snorted.

Brent's face was a study in commiseration. "When do you have to go back?"

Oh, but didn't he sound calm and in control? Jen suppressed an evil grin. Now that she knew what she could do to him and exactly how to do it, she couldn't wait for a chance to jerk that composure right back out from under him. Feminine power was a heady brew.

"Today. Damn fool's only gonna be in town until nine tonight."

Brent glanced at his watch. "It's almost noon now. Might be tough to get a flight out."

"Clancy'll find me something. Kid may not look

like much, but he's got brains and grit." Williamson seemed to think about that for a minute. Either that, or he was captivated by the glowing tip of his cigar. Finally, he blinked and looked up at Brent. "Like I said before, I wanted to talk to you about something."

Brent raised an eyebrow. "What's that?"

"It's kind of a business proposition." Bill rolled his cigar between thumb and forefinger. "See, what I'd like you to think about—"

"Mr. Williamson! Mr. Williamson!" Clancy raced around the corner in a Jerry Lewis welter of arms and legs, skidding to a halt in the face of his boss's glower.

"What is it now, boy?"

"I got you a reservation, but the flight leaves LAX at two, so we'll have to get going right away." Looking more worried than ever, Clancy fidgeted with his tie again.

"Well, hell." Williamson jammed a hand on one hip and dropped his chin to his chest, muttering into his vest. "All right, Clancy, get in the car and get your motor running. I'll be right there." Clancy scrambled off.

"Boy might have brains and grit, but he's as nervous as a long-tail cat in a room full of rockers." Shaking his head, Williamson turned back to Brent. "Look, Maddox, I've got to get going or that Clancy'll pitch a fit and step right in it. But I still want to talk to you. How 'bout I give you a call tomorrow?"

"Fine with me." Brent slipped a thin gold case out of his pocket and extracted a business card. "I'll be at this number all day."

"Good enough." Bill tucked the card away, then startled Jen by reaching out to seize her hand and give it a single robust shake. After which, he grabbed Brent's hand and pumped even more vigorously. "You take good care of this little lady, now, you hear? I'll be in touch." He chuckled knowingly. "You folks get on back to your . . . celebratin'."

"Thanks, Bill." As soon as Williamson disappeared around the corner, Brent turned back to Jen. The look in his eyes could have melted asbestos. "Now, where were we?"

"Damn!"

Juggling a copper saucepan, a gallon jug of milk, a mug, a giant, economy-size can of cocoa, and a huge bag of marshmallows, Brent suspected he may have bitten off more than he could carry. When he dropped the heavy pot on his foot, he was sure of it.

"Ouch! *Shhhhhhh!*"

He deposited his remaining paraphernalia on the gleaming butcher-block table. Creeping over to retrieve the saucepan, he darted a furtive glance at the door to Crampton's quarters. Why did the damned architect have to put the housekeeper's rooms right off the kitchen? Feeling idiotically like an intruder in his own house, he tiptoed over to the huge gas range and eased the pot onto a front burner. It took him a little longer to figure out how the stove worked, but he persevered.

Five minutes later he'd managed to locate a spoon and a measuring cup and had the ingredients—at least he was pretty sure they were the right ingredients—in the pan ready to go.

He was a desperate man.

Sleepless nights were getting to be a habit. A few

more and he'd turn into a zombie. Or was that a vampire? Either way, it couldn't go on.

He only hoped hot chocolate would do the soporific trick, sex sure as hell wasn't helping much. And if he fixed himself a drink every time he got to thinking about Jen and couldn't sleep, he'd be an alcoholic before she went back to Donnerton.

Strike that last bit. He didn't even want to think about Jen going back.

He stirred the cocoa mixture carefully so the spoon wouldn't clang against the pan. At this point anything was worth a try.

"You want something?"

He yelped and nearly jumped out of his skin. Spinning around, he clapped a hand over his hammering heart. Much to his disgust, it turned out to be the hand that held the spoon. He glanced down then back up, glaring at Althea Crampton as muddy rivulets trickled down his bare chest. "Quit sneaking up on me, dammit!"

Except for a raised eyebrow, her customary stone face didn't alter, but he could have sworn Crampton Bligh was laughing at him. Which was ridiculous, of course, because that would mean the woman actually had a sense of humor. Still, he couldn't shake the feeling that he'd managed to amuse her, so he scowled suspiciously.

"You want something?" she repeated blandly. She *was* laughing at him, he was sure of it. But sneakily, without cracking a smile, so he couldn't call her on it.

"Cocoa," he muttered, turning back to his cooking. "I couldn't sleep."

"Hot milk."

He slid a glance over his shoulder. She looked

different in her no-nonsense nightgown and matching blue robe, her gray hair roped in a braid over her shoulder. Kind of . . . human.

Confused by the transformation, he directed his attention back to the stove. "I hate the taste of hot milk."

"You forgot the sugar."

He frowned down at the simmering liquid. Strange clots had started to congeal on the surface. "Sugar?"

While he was distracted a capable hand reached around to steal his spoon. With all the gentleness of a Sherman tank, his housekeeper nudged him aside, usurping his place at the stove. Fuming impotently about too many cooks spoiling the chocolate, he watched her spoon up a sample.

"Too much milk. Heat's too high. No sugar." So saying, she marched across the room and dumped all his hard work down the drain.

"Hey! Wait a minute—"

"Sit."

"But I—"

"Sit down."

Well, since she put it like that . . .

He plopped down in one of the chairs at the table where the staff took their meals, grumpily plucking up a napkin to dab at his sticky chest. Crampton expertly whipped up a new batch of cocoa, with sugar, he noted sourly. Sulking like a kid stuck in a corner, he pressed his lips in a sullen line and brooded about the way women liked to lord over a man.

Throwing out his cooking. Bossing him around. Keeping him off balance. Making love with a guy when all he wanted was great sex. Telling him they were proud of him and making him go all sappy inside.

Brent hadn't been proud of much in the last few years. Not that he'd done anything to be ashamed of, he assured himself virtuously, but he hadn't accomplished a whole lot, either.

Hope Away from Home was a different story. The concept was his baby from start to finish. He was the one who found backers to get it off the ground, he organized and headed the Hope Foundation. He even designed the structural alterations that made the houses user-friendly.

Not that he thought he was indispensable. He didn't, not for a minute. An army of hardworking people donated both their time and money to Hope, and he would never have made it this far without their help. If he died tomorrow, Hope would go on without him.

The work was important. He wasn't in it for the glory and tried to keep his name out of things as much as possible. But down deep inside where it was personal, he was proud of his work.

"Why can't you sleep this time?"

"Hmm?" Caught up in his own musings, he answered automatically. "Oh, this morning. Jen said she was proud of me."

"And that keeps you awake?" He didn't have to see her face to know that she was amused again.

"Yes," he muttered grudgingly. "That and a few other things." Like the way Jen felt about him. The way he might or might not feel about her. And what the hell he was going to do about it all.

"I like her."

Brent clamped his fingers around the edge of the

table, but almost fell out of his chair anyway. Crampton had never, ever admitted to liking anybody before.

"You do?" Brow furrowed, he pondered this astounding revelation. "Why?"

"She's not like the rest of them."

Two conversations in one week. Althea was getting downright chatty these days. Brent wondered if he'd ever get used to the garrulous side of Bligh. "The rest of them?"

"Those floozies you usually bring around here."

"Floozies?" Being a man who valued his life, he strangled the guffaw threatening to burst from his chest.

"That's what I said. Floozies."

Crampton neatly poured chocolate into the mug. To his renewed amazement, she got a second cup, poured some cocoa for herself, and joined him at the table. She was being sociable. Maybe he was dreaming. Just to make sure, he reached down to surreptitiously pinch his thigh. It hurt. "Why do you call them floozies?"

The housekeeper sniffed disdainfully and dropped two marshmallows into each cup. "Not a thought in their heads but getting their hair and nails done or which dress they're going to wear."

Uncomfortable with her killingly accurate assessment of the women he usually dated, he shifted in his chair. "That's not—"

She skewered him with a rapier look. "Money. That's what the floozies want from a man like you."

Stung because she was right, he sipped his cocoa and mumbled, "For all you know, that's what Jen Casey wants too." Of course, he knew it wasn't true.

By the sardonic look on her face, Althea knew it too. "That girl's crazy about you."

"Maybe."

"No maybe about it." Her eyes never left his face as she lifted her own mug and drank. She plunked it down and glared. "So what are you going to do about it?"

"Do?" Unable to meet her penetrating, expectant stare, he dropped his gaze to his own cup. He poked at a marshmallow, making it bob in the chocolate.

She was happy to clarify. "You gonna let that girl get away?"

Since his mouth had suddenly gone dry, he drank again. "I don't know."

"Pitiful," Althea decided, and he flinched. "You love her?"

Now, *that* was blunt. "I don't know," he mumbled a second time. "I've been thinking about that."

"You think too much," declared Crampton, and his eyes lifted warily to her face.

"You can't think too much."

"Yes," his housekeeper corrected, "you can." And she chugged the rest of her chocolate, marshmallows and all.

Standing, she marched across to the sink to wash the dishes. She stowed the cocoa ingredients with practiced efficiency. It didn't take her long to tidy up. He expected her to depart in her customary black cloud of silence, but she stopped at the entrance to her quarters and looked over her shoulder.

"Sometimes you just have to feel," she said, and closed the door behind her with an assertive snap.

Brent stared at that closed door for a long, long

time. His marshmallows melted away. His chocolate got cold. The sun started to come up.

Sometimes you just have to feel.

Well, hell.

So much for soul-searching, analyzing, and agonizing.

Unfortunately, it was easier to talk about turning off the thought processes than to do it. His off-analysis switch stubbornly refused to flip. The preference for reason over emotion was probably a man thing, something to do with the Y-chromosome, he guessed.

Still, there was no question that logic had let him down this time. Approaching his relationship with Jen rationally hadn't gotten him anywhere but agitated and confused. Somehow, he would have to ignore the questions he'd been stockpiling and let go of his doubts and fears. Dump all those worrisome ifs, ands, and buts.

Sometimes you just have to feel.

Okay, he could do that. Feeling self-conscious and stupid, he shifted in his chair and concentrated on emptying his mind. Smoothing out all those interfering, perfectly understandable concerns, and releasing them. It took a while—and surprised the hell out of him—but he was finally able to do it. His mind was blessedly blank for the first time in days. Weeks. Maybe even months.

And he did feel. In fact, he felt a couple of things.

First of all, peace. It wafted in like the calm after a bad storm, filling up all the restless, uncertain holes in his soul.

Barreling in right on its heels came a big, bubbly, ain't-that-a-kick-in-the-ass emotion. It tumbled straight out of his heart, dragging happiness in its wake, expanding in his chest like a hot-air balloon. All of a sudden he knew, just knew, he could leap tall buildings in a single bound. Or perform all kinds of other impossible feats. Like fly to the moon. Or farther.

He loved her. Of course he loved her. Any idiot could see that.

His smile started small, then grew and grew. Finally, he threw back his head and laughed out loud. "God bless you, Althea Crampton!" he shouted.

Through the door he heard a brisk but muffled, "Go to bed."

TWELVE

Casting a cautious look from side to side, Jen skulked around a corner and up the stairs. She slunk down the hallway hugging the far-right wall.

Down on the first floor a door opened, then closed. She paused and cocked her head, listening. When the footsteps moved toward the back of the house, she stole farther down the hall, stopping in front of Mrs. Maddox's bedroom. Peeking around the doorjamb, she reconnoitered. Empty.

Easing over the threshold, she tiptoed across the presumably Aubusson carpet. As her fingers closed around the knob on the bathroom door, her heart pounded giddily in her breast. *You should've taken a minute to come up with a plausible excuse for being here*, she chided herself, but twisted the knob anyway and swung open the door.

A long, quiet breath eased out between her parted lips. She didn't need an excuse after all. Nobody was there.

"Good." She was alone. Completely alone. She

dashed back across the bedroom and closed the door, then made a beeline for the telephone.

Tomorrow was her last day with Brent. She needed advice, she thought desperately, and started punching buttons. From an expert. Specifically, she needed to learn how a woman went about exposing her innermost feelings without making a total fool of herself.

The number rang once. Twice. "Come on, come on," she muttered urgently. A third ring. Lord, what if nobody was home?

"Hello."

"Candy?"

A pause. Then slowly, suspiciously: "Who is this?"

"It's me."

"Who's me?"

With an exasperated roll of her eyes, Jen cupped a hand around the mouthpiece, flicking a nervous glance toward the door. "Me. Jen."

"Jen? Jen Casey?"

Well, how many Jens did Candy know? Honestly! "Yes," she hissed.

"What's wrong with your voice?"

I don't have time for this! "Nothing's wrong with my voice!"

"Then why are you whispering?"

Jen squeezed her eyes shut and prayed God would deliver her from knuckleheaded friends. "Because I don't want anybody to hear me," she explained with exaggerated patience.

Candy lowered her own voice. "Oh. What's going on?"

Pinching the bridge of her nose between thumb

and forefinger, Jen bit back an unladylike oath. "Candy, *you* don't have to whisper. Nobody can hear you but me."

"Oh. Oh, yeah." Candy's voice recovered its normal volume. "What's going on?"

"I need your advice."

"My advice? Sure thing. On what?"

Jen smiled fondly. It wouldn't occur to Candy that she might not have any useful advice to contribute; she was always ready and willing to contribute anyway. But sometimes she knew what she was talking about.

"Jen? On what?"

She'd already decided there was no way she was going to get out of this without answering a lot of excruciatingly personal questions, but Jen allowed herself a brief, wistful wish that her privacy could be spared.

"Jen? Are you still there?"

"I need your advice on . . . well . . . okay." Best to get this over quickly. Taking a deep breath, she whispered in a rush, "I've gotten kind of involved with Brent." Who would have guessed she had this incredible gift for understatement?

"Involved?"

The slow, leading intonation had Jen grimacing. "Yes, involved."

"How involved?"

"Very involved. You might even say *deeply* involved."

Candy paused a third time. "Are we talking all the way involved here, Jen? As in *all the way?*"

That's when Jen discovered that one could, indeed, blush long-distance. Pressing her lips together, she nodded jerkily.

"You aren't by any chance nodding your head, are you, Jen?"

Feeling stupid now as well as embarrassed, Jen cleared her throat. "Yes."

"Yes, you're nodding your head, or yes, you're all the way involved with Brent Maddox?"

"Both," she snapped, then dropped her voice back to a whisper. "Both."

"Hmm." There was a leer in that *hmm*, Jen was sure of it. The fourth pause was the longest yet. The exultant whoop that ended it nearly shattered Jen's eardrum. "All right, Jennifer Marie! Way to go, girl!"

"Candy."

Jen wasn't particularly surprised when her whisper failed to register through the ensuing round of ribald congratulations. She tried again, sotto voce. "Candy."

When that didn't work either, she smiled nastily, pulled the receiver away from her ear, and jabbed the pound button three times, producing a satisfying trio of high-pitched beeps.

In spite of the intervening six inches, Candy's curse came through loud and clear.

"Are you with me now?" Jen whispered sweetly.

"Dammit, Jen, that was low. Really low." Candy huffed, then grumbled, "Okay, I'm with you so far. You and Brent are lovers."

Trust Candy to cut through the euphemisms. "Yes." Jen swallowed. "Actually, it's a little more complicated than that. I love him," she whisper-blurted before her courage failed her.

"You. Love. Him. Oh. My. God," Candy

breathed. Then urgently: "Does he love you too? Does he?"

"I don't know. Maybe." Jen's chin shot up, and she forgot all about whispering. "He darned well better love me, if he knows what's good for him!"

"Jen, Jen, Jen." Candy tsk-tsked into the phone. "You haven't told him yet, have you?"

"No."

"Why not?"

Surely that was obvious. "Well, because I don't know how to go about it. I never told a man I loved him before." Candy, on the other hand, was a pro when it came to falling in and out of love. "That's where you come in."

"You want *me* to tell him?"

Jen barely resisted the urge to jump up and beat her head against the wall. "No, I do not want you to tell him. I want you to tell *me* how to tell him."

"You're putting me on, right?"

"Look, will you just shut up and tell me?" Okay, so it wasn't the most logically worded request. She was under a lot of pressure here.

"All right, all right. Calm down," Candy soothed. "Now, as I understand it, you want to tell Brent Maddox you love him, but you don't know how to do it. Right?"

Relieved because the conversation was finally moving in the right direction, Jen nodded crisply. "Right."

"Right. Okay, let's take this one step at a time. Step number one. You and Brent are alone."

Where was a pencil when you needed one? "Alone," Jen repeated.

"Good. Step number two. You slide your arms around his neck and look deeply into his eyes."

"Arms around the neck, look into his eyes. Got it." Hearing a suspicious gurgle, Jen scowled. "Candy Johnson, are you laughing at me?"

"No! No, of course not. I just had something stuck in my throat." The throat in question was dutifully cleared. "There. See? Much better. Now, where were we? Oh yeah, you're looking deeply into his eyes. You give him a long, juicy kiss. . . ."

Oh, good. Kissing Brent was one of her favorite things. His lips were so warm, so firm. God, she got chills just *thinking* about his lips! Caught up in the scenario, Jen let herself imagine the way his tongue would duel with hers. Her toes curled into tight little knots in her sandals. "A *long*, juicy kiss. Yeah. Then what?"

"Then you say . . ."

"I say . . ."

"You say, 'Brent, I love you.' "

"Yeah, I say—" Jen's brows snapped together. "That's it? 'Brent, I love you'? That's the best you can do?"

"Hey, pal, when it comes to words, they don't come any better than those."

Thinking about it, Jen decided that this was one of the few times Candy might know what she was talking about. Suddenly she found herself smiling. "No, I guess they don't. Thanks, Candy."

"Anytime, anytime." Candy was clearly a humble, yet magnanimous expert. "Just be sure to let me know how things turn out. Good luck, honey. Give him hell."

"Only if he gives me the wrong response."

◆━━━━━━━◆

This is silly, Jen scolded herself. *I've been naked with the man, for goodness' sake. There's no reason to feel over-exposed now.*

Of course, they *were* outside. The sun was shining. And Brent had that you'll-be-naked-again-before-you-know-it gleam in his eye.

"Forget it," she told him. "I'm not making love on the beach in broad daylight." Settling herself on the blanket, she tugged up the bodice of her new bathing suit. If the thighs were cut any higher, she wouldn't have a bodice to tug.

"Did I say anything about making love?" he asked innocently. Sprawled across the blanket wearing nothing but brief black Speedos, a great tan, and a come-hither smile, he looked about as innocent as Al Capone.

"You were thinking it."

He chuckled. "Can't help it, sweetheart. I think about you, I think about making love. I see you, I think about making love." He reached over to trace a finger down one of her straps. His voice dropped seductively. "I touch you, I think about making love."

Steadfastly ignoring the slow burn that touch ignited, she swatted his hand away. "Oh no, you don't." She was determined to tell him she loved him and coax—or coerce—him into telling her he felt the same. She'd never be able to do it if he laid hands on her. "You just lie there and work on your tan."

"Yes, ma'am." He talked a meek game, but she didn't trust that Cheshire-cat grin for a second. She kept an eagle eye on him until he lay back and closed his eyes.

Assuming the sunbathing position herself, she thought about full circles, and smiled. Sunbathing was where this whole thing started. Of course tanning was easier this time around, because she had something to think about besides how long it would take. She had to review her game plan and work up the nerve to see it through.

It took about twenty minutes to do both, then she rolled onto her side, facing him. "Brent?"

"Hmm?"

On a deep breath for courage, she slid closer. Leaning over him, she slid her hands up his chest and behind his neck. She was almost lying on top of him.

His eyes stayed closed, but the grin slithered back as his arm slid around her waist. "I thought you said—"

"I did." Too late, it occurred to her that she'd already made a tactical error. She should have started the kiss in an upright position. Being prone on top of Brent made straight thinking almost impossible. For one thing, she could feel his heart beating against hers. For another, that magnificent, hairy chest rubbed against her with every breath they took.

Well, it was too late to back out now. She'd just have to concentrate harder. "Brent?"

"I'm still here, honey."

You give him a long, juicy kiss, look deeply into his eyes, and say, "Brent, I love you." Okay, check. First the kiss. Another deep breath for courage, and Jen lowered her lips to his.

Her tongue stroked across his mouth, slipping inside when he opened. The growl of approval started deep in his chest and vibrated clear through her. He tightened his arms and pulled her completely on top of him, shifting his legs so she lay between his thighs. One big hand stroked up her back to cradle her head while he deepened the kiss.

He was still kissing her when he rolled her underneath him, but he lifted his lips long enough to groan, "Oh, baby, what you do to me."

Now. Tell him now. "Brent, I—"

"God. I know, I know." He swooped for another kiss, and his hand slid down to cover her breast. The last two words of her four-word script exploded into thought confetti.

"You've got a phone call."

Brent went utterly still and lifted his lips. His eyes closed briefly before snapping open to special-deliver a deadly glare to Althea Crampton. "Tell them I'm busy."

The housekeeper didn't budge. Up to her ankles in sand, she stood with her hands on her hips. "It's Williamson. You said to tell you if he called." Her eyes narrowed. "So I'm telling you."

"Damn." He closed his eyes again, obviously struggling for control. When he opened them to look down at Jen, the fires were banked but not extinguished. "Sorry, sweetheart."

Torn between abject embarrassment at being caught in a thoroughly compromising situation and acute frustration at not being thoroughly compromised, Jen mumbled, "It's okay. I understand."

"Yeah, well . . ." He leaned down to give her another quick, hard kiss, and she groaned. "Hold that thought." He climbed to his feet and jogged up the beach after the retreating Crampton Bligh.

Hold that thought? Sure. What thought?

❖―――❖

"Maddox, that you, boy?"

Brent took a deep breath and tried to repress the impatience in his voice. "Hello, Bill. Yes, it's me. What can I do for you?" Whatever it was, he meant to do it quickly. He had a beautiful woman waiting for him.

He swiveled his chair toward the picture window behind him. Unfortunately, it opened on the rolling lawns in front of the house, which meant he couldn't see the blanket he and Jen had spread out on the sand. But he could still see her in his mind's eye wearing that racy swimsuit he'd talked her into letting him buy yesterday afternoon. The woman did look good in fire-engine red, cut high at the thigh.

"Hold on a second, will you? I've just got to—" The voice on the other end became muffled. "No, no, Clancy, don't—" A loud crash followed. "Dammit, boy, I told you not to climb up on that thing!"

"Bill?" Brent waited, only vaguely aware of the clatter and curses on the other end. Nine tenths of his brain was back on the beach, reliving the kiss the phone call had interrupted. If that kiss had been an earthquake, it would have registered at least seven-point-nine on the Richter scale.

Brent shifted uncomfortably in his chair. If it had been anybody but Bill Williamson on the line, he would consign the call straight to hell. The fact that he respected the crusty old oil man who devoted more time to charity than he did to his wells gave him the patience to wait.

But not, he hoped, for long.

"Sorry about that. Kid's book-smart, but he's got

no more horse sense than—" The sentence ended in a long-suffering sigh. "Look, Maddox, I don't have much time. I just wanted to make my offer so you could think it over and get back to me in the next couple of days."

"What offer is that, Bill?"

"Why, job offer, a' course, what'd you think?"

Nonplussed, Brent swung the chair around to face his desk. "You want to offer me a job?"

"Didn't I just say so?"

Talk about your hard lefts. *What gave him the idea I wanted to join the nine-to-five set?* Brent shook his head. "What kind of job?"

"Frank Ketchum—you know Frank, don't you? Our western region executive director?"

"Yeah. Little guy with a goatee."

"Right. Well, Frank's doc tells him he's got to retire, or the old ticker's gonna up and quit on him. Thought you might be interested in taking his place?"

"Me?" Confused, Brent said the first thing that came to mind. "Why would you want me?" The fact that he honestly couldn't think of a single reason shocked him more than the fact that he'd asked in the first place.

Williamson's snort seemed to say that *that* was the dumbest question he'd ever heard. "Dumbest question I ever heard. We've had our eye on you, son, and I've got to tell you, we like what we see. Oh, I know you don't like to talk about it, but you've done a passel of good work in the last few years. When we saw the way you buckled down and got that Hope project going, we knew you were the right man for the job."

Brent's lips twisted sardonically. "I think you're

giving me too much credit, Bill. I didn't do all that stuff alone, you know." But his heart raced, driven by something that felt like hope. And if that wasn't the craziest—

"Well, hell, boy, movin' and shakin' is what that directorship is all about. Didn't I say we knew you were the right man for the job? Board voted unanimously."

"Unanimously? But I—"

"Salary's not much to speak of."

They wanted to give him money too? "I don't need—"

" 'Course you don't. Folks like you and me need more money like an ape needs more ugly. Just throw you into a higher tax bracket, that's all. Damned feds." Williamson let that hang for a second before continuing jovially, "Bright young fella like you just needs somethin' to keep him off the streets at night."

The line was delivered with a chuckle, but Brent had the sudden, unsettling feeling that the old man understood him better than he understood himself. "I guess."

"There you go. Regional office is right there in Los Angeles, so that makes things handy. Hell, you won't even have to relocate."

"Right. Handy," Brent murmured dazedly. But it was the original premise that still had his brain scrambling to catch up. *A job?*

"Frank's retiring on September first. You give it some thought and call me back. Don't wait too long, though. If you don't want the job, we're gonna be runnin' our tails off tryin' to find somebody else."

He wanted to laugh, wanted to tell Williamson to get serious. But the words stuck somewhere in his throat. What came out was, "Sure. I'll let you know. Bye, Bill."

More bewildered than ever, Brent hung up. The whole conversation was a swan dive into the Twilight Zone. What in the hell did he need with a job?

Screwiest damned idea he'd ever heard in his life.

So why wasn't he laughing?

Striding down the beach, Brent looked like a man who had things on his mind. Since his expression was one part pensive frown, one part baffled scowl, and zero parts sexy smile, Jen had a hunch romance wasn't one of those things. She huffed out a disappointed breath. Well, darn. Now she'd have to start all over again.

But when he dropped down on the blanket and looped an arm around her waist, he preoccupation was so obvious, even *she* forgot to think about romance. Scooting closer, she peered up at him. "Brent? What is it?"

"Screwiest damned idea I've ever heard."

"What's the screwiest da—uh, idea you've ever heard?"

"He offered me a job."

Her eyes widened. "Bill Williamson offered you a job?" Still staring out at the ocean, Brent nodded. "With United Charities? What kind of job?"

"Western region executive director."

Jen wasn't exactly sure what a western region executive director did, but one thing was clear. "Wow. That's some offer."

"Yeah." His perplexed blue gaze swung to her face. "But why'd he offer it to me?"

A simple question, if it hadn't been loaded with total bewilderment. "What do you mean?"

"I don't need a job, for one thing."

"Hmm." She wasn't convinced, but they'd get back to that in a minute. "And for the other?"

Brent glanced away as one broad shoulder lifted in a negligent *I could care less.* Jen might have believed it, except his fingers had clamped around her waist. "What makes him think I can handle it? I haven't held down a job in twelve years. And busing tables at the Blue Anchor isn't exactly your standard executive training."

Here was her chance to do for him what he'd already done for her—give him a clearer view of both himself and all the possibilities. "Oh, I don't know. You were a very high-powered busboy. Quick. Ambitious. Maybe even driven." He snorted, and she grinned. "Did you ask Williamson why he wanted you?"

"Yeah." Brent cleared his throat, looking adorably embarrassed. "He, uh, said something about my work on Hope Away from Home and a few other projects."

"Uh-huh. Sounds like the stuff executive directors are made of to me. Don't you think you could handle those same kinds of projects for United Charities?"

"Sure. I guess." He grimaced. "I'm not much on nine-to-five."

She rolled her eyes. "Who is? But some jobs are worth the hassle."

"Hmm." His eyes narrowed on her face. "You think I should take it, don't you?" She smiled. "Why?"

"I want you to be happy."

Eyebrows raised, he asked, "And assuming I'm not, you think this job will make a difference?"

Jen gave him a get-real look. "Aren't you forgetting something? I've seen you in action, buster. Schmoozing big bucks at charity benefits, talking logistics and planning with Williamson, pitching Hope Away from Home. You live for wheeling and dealing."

His lips quirked. "Think so?"

"Know so. There's a lot of 'let's get the job done' in your makeup, fella. Perfectly understandable, of course."

"Is it?"

"Well, sure. You might run with the hotshot jet set these days, but your roots are strictly small town, same as mine, and they're sunk smack dab in the work ethic."

"I've come a long ways from Donnerton, Jen."

"In some ways," she conceded. "Not so far in others. You know what they say."

Brent looked to heaven. "Wait a minute—she'll tell us."

" 'You can take the boy out of the middle class, but you can't take the middle class out of the boy.' "

"That is not what they say."

"I'm improvising here. Work with me. The sentiment is valid."

"Hmm." He tilted his head. "You *do* think I should take the job. Don't you?"

Jen batted her lashes. "Gosh, Brent, don't ask me, that's entirely your decision. I wouldn't dream of interfering."

He gave a rough bark of laughter right before he

toppled her back onto the blanket. "I'll think about it."

Later that night Brent had to admit Jen had him pegged. He did like to wheel and deal and get the job done. So why not do what he liked on a regular basis? Hell, he'd been on vacation for the last twelve years. Maybe it was time he did something productive.

The more he thought about the whole thing, the better it sounded. Jen and Bill were right—he had the know-how. God only knew he had the time. Why not put both to good use?

But in the end, it wasn't the logic that convinced him. It was the excitement that sprang up after it. Williamson had understood, and now Brent did too. He'd been wrong, he did need the directorship. Needed it bone-deep for his pride and self-respect.

So the next morning he called Bill to tell him he'd take the job.

"Well now, that's fine, son," chortled Williamson. "Real fine. Glad to have you. I'll give Ketchum a call and have him set up a meet. Next week all right?"

"Fine. Talk to you then, Bill." Brent hung up and kicked back in his chair, crossing his feet on the desktop. Folding his hands across his stomach, he thought about the changes the past week had wrought in his life. They were almost too radical to take in.

In a few weeks he'd have a career he enjoyed, doing something worthwhile, something he was good at. Best of all, he'd earned the job—beat silver-platter hiring all to hell.

He was in love with a sweet, sexy woman who could care less whether or not he had a dollar to his name, let alone a few million of them. Being well on his way to becoming a card-carrying member of productive society blew away all the reasons he'd given himself for keeping his distance.

He could have her. For life.

Heart pounding, mouth suddenly dry, Brent pulled his feet off the desk and sat up slowly. For life. As in he could marry Jen Casey. The idea sent him to his feet, hands fisted at his sides. He could ask Jen Casey to marry him.

The trick would be getting her to overlook his money and say yes.

The woman loved him. Of course she'd say yes.

Probably.

Brent's jaw set with resolve. Oh, she'd say yes, all right. If she didn't say it the first time, he'd just refuse to take her home and keep on asking. She'd come around. Sooner or later.

THIRTEEN

It was the worst case of pussyfooting around she'd ever seen. But she couldn't seem to stop.

Come on, Jennifer, three little words. How hard can that be? Plenty hard, if the last twenty-four hours were any indication. Her every attempt to tell Brent how she felt had been a washout. Pathetic.

Out of the corner of her eye, she watched him take a sip of wine and heard the clink when he set the glass on the coffee table. He straightened his shoulders and shifted on the low-slung leather sofa to face her. Reluctantly, she met his gaze. He obviously had something to say. Hopefully, it wasn't good-bye.

He took a deep breath. "Jen, I—" He broke off, coughing slightly and picking up his glass again. "How was the crab?"

With an inner sigh—relief or disappointment?—she forced her twisting fingers to stop. Smiled brightly. "Oh. It was delicious. Just . . . delicious."

Washed in the soft glow cast by the chrome floor lamp, she imagined her face read like an open book.

Love, hope, and *Please don't send me away*. She gazed at him helplessly for long seconds before she fell back on finger twisting.

"So you liked it. Good. That's . . . good."

Yeah, swell.

A minute or two later Brent put down the glass again, slid a little closer, and took her hand. Nice move, she admitted silently. "Listen, Jen, I wanted—"

She leaned forward slightly, waiting, wondering if Brent could hear her quick, expectant heartbeat. "What did you want, Brent?" she asked softly.

He reached up with his free hand to tuck a lock of hair behind her ear. His fingers trailed down her cheek. "I wanted to ask you—" He paused, then dropped his hand. "Did I tell you I decided to take the job?"

Her shoulders drooped imperceptibly. It was all she could do not to close her eyes and wipe a weary hand down her face. He'd been about to say something else, she was sure of it. Something she'd give her right arm to hear, or be able to say herself.

She managed to keep the chagrin out of her voice when she answered, "Yes, you did. It's a wonderful opportunity. I know you'll be the best western region executive director United Charities ever had."

"Yeah?"

"Yes."

If at first you don't succeed, she reminded herself, and screwed up the courage to try again. "Uh, Brent . . ." She moistened her lips, thrilled when his eyes heated and tracked the progress of her tongue. Things were looking up. "Brent, yesterday on the beach, I wanted to tell you how I feel, that is, how much I . . . but then we kind of got, uh, carried away and I couldn't think. . . ."

A promising start. Infuriatingly, it faltered and faded away unfinished. Jen swore silently. *I'm making a grade-A mess of this.*

Where was Cupid when you needed him? Left on their own, she and Brent would probably dance around the point until the cows came home. Time was running out. If she didn't stop making calf eyes at the man and get down to business, she'd wind up back in Donnerton nursing a broken heart a few hours from now.

That possibility had her jaw firming. *Oh, no I won't.*

Jen stirred, her posture changing subtly as her spine straightened with resolution. Inching closer to Brent, she slowly reached up to twine her arms around his neck and urged his head down to hers. Her lips skimmed lightly over his once, then once again. Her fingers crept up his nape, tangled in his hair. Their lips met.

She kissed him like there was no tomorrow.

Because there might not be.

Brent growled and wrapped his arms around her, crushing her up against him. The kiss went on and on. Jen wasn't sure she could breathe through the lip-lock, but who cared? Hazily, she reminded herself to break it up soon and say what needed to be said before Brent dragged her off to bed. She couldn't take much more of this. And boy, was it getting warm in here!

By the time they pulled apart, they were both breathing raggedly.

Her hands slid out of his hair to rest on his shoulders. Taking a shaky little breath, she looked up at him. "Brent—" She paused to clear the hoarseness out of her throat. "Brent, I love you."

There was complete silence while her trembling heart hung in the balance. Then he lunged.

"Oh God, Jen," he groaned, snatching her close. "I know you do. I know. I love you too." They kissed again. It was wild and sweet, and turned her blood thick and hot.

"Well now." Gasping, they jerked apart and turned to find Althea Crampton silhouetted in the dimly lit hallway between living room and dining room. In the weak light, her expression looked both sentimental and flustered. Her face didn't wear the combination comfortably.

She slipped a handkerchief from her apron pocket and dabbed at her eyes. "Well. Took you two long enough, but you managed to get it done in the end."

Brent scowled. "Althea—"

The housekeeper ignored him, pinning Jen with one of her patented gimlet stares. "Boy can be a handful, no mistake. Too many admirers chasing after him."

"Hey!" The "boy" sounded indignant.

In spite of the need thrumming through her, Jen's lips twitched. "Is that right?"

Althea nodded curtly. "Lots of floozies and bloodsuckers out there just itching to get their hooks in him. But he's a bright man—a word or two of advice usually does the trick."

"I'll keep that in mind," Jen assured her solemnly. But her body was humming. *Please go away, Althea, I'm dying here.*

The woman was obviously a mind reader, because

she said, "See that you do," and turned toward the kitchen, shoving her handkerchief into her pocket and patting her hair as she trundled off.

"What was that all about?" muttered Brent.

Men! They could be so slow. Anybody with eyes in her head could see that Althea Crampton considered herself much more than Brent's housekeeper. Jen looped her arms around his waist and tried to tug him closer. "She's been looking after you for a long time."

Brent glanced over her head at the empty archway, brow furrowed. "Crampton Bligh looking after me? What are you talking about?"

Talk didn't interest Jen, action did. So she said, "I'll explain later," hooked her hands over his shoulders, and pressed against him invitingly.

"Yeah," he growled, "later." Their lips met. The mingled tastes of wine and Brent had her head swimming lazily as she wrapped herself around him.

Drunk with lust, she tore her lips away from his and trailed kisses along his jaw and down his neck. "Say it again."

"I love you." He grabbed a handful of her hair and dragged her back to his mouth. "I'll always love you," he murmured against her lips, and smothered them with his.

She opened and his tongue slid in to fence with hers. On a desperate moan she tightened her arms around his neck, trying to get closer. Closer? She'd crawl right inside him if she could. *He loved her!*

He pulled back, nipped at her bottom lip, nibbled his way over to her ear. She tilted her head to one side to give him better access. His teeth closed on her earlobe and she gasped. "I love you too. You'll never know how much."

His lips crushed hers again in a kiss that sizzled straight to the soles of her feet. Somehow she ended up on his lap, one of his big hands cupping her head. His tongue plunged and retreated—over and over again. His other hand streaked up under her bodice to knead her breast, and desire tore up her throat in a frantic groan.

"Jesus." Brent shot to his feet, cradling her in his arms as he strode out of the room and carried her up the stairs. Jen fumbled open the top two buttons of his shirt and pressed wet kisses across his collarbone. He shuddered, his arms tightening.

She licked his neck. "Hurry."

His rough bark of laughter sounded more than a little strained. "I am, sweetheart. Believe me, I am."

Maybe. But just to make sure, she flicked her tongue over the pulse hammering at the base of his throat.

"God." He surged through the bedroom door, shoving it closed with his elbow. A second later he dropped her onto the bed and came down on top of her. His weight pressed her into the mattress. It felt good, but not good enough.

He rose on one elbow to unbutton her blouse. Jen bit back a frustrated curse. Who had time for buttons? Didn't the man recognize dire straits when he saw them? She gave his shoulder a hefty shove, flipping him onto his back. He was in the middle of his "What are you—" when she straddled him and yanked at his belt.

"Yeah. Oh, yeah." While she struggled with his zipper he swept the skirt of her green sundress up to her waist and tore off her panties. A fierce little thrill zipped up her spine.

Then he was in her hand, hot and smooth, hard and ready. And she was in *his* hand, throbbing and aching to be filled. Rising up on her knees, she positioned herself.

Brent rasped, "Wait!"

Wait? No way! She started to sink down on him, had in fact claimed just the first inch of heaven, when he grabbed her waist and brought progress to an unwelcome halt.

His eyes were closed, his chest working like a bellows, but he still managed to say, "God, baby. Wait." He swallowed heavily and gasped, "Just let me get—" One of his hands flailed blindly toward the nightstand.

Wrapped as she was in a needy haze, it took a minute for his meaning to penetrate. This time Jen did curse. Exactly what she had in mind, she thought wildly, lunging for the drawer. Lucky for him, she wanted all their children to be planned. It gave her the patience to rip open the packet and roll the protection over him. His hips surged eagerly.

"Now." His voice was guttural. He grabbed her around the waist and lifted her over him again.

She sank as he lunged upward, fusing their bodies in a single movement. It was so perfect, so exquisitely perfect, that for a moment they froze, their ragged breaths tearing lightly through the quiet room.

Their gazes held as she braced her hands against his sweat-damp blue chambray shirt and started to move up and down. Slowly at first. Then faster, and faster still. She watched him climb, knowing he watched too. It was unbearably exciting. Her head dropped back and she started to close her eyes.

"No," he growled, and drove into her again. "No, watch. Watch us, baby. I want you to see it happen."

Her skirt was bunched in his fists. She followed his gaze down to where their bodies joined. His hips pumped. She saw him enter, felt him fill her. It was the most erotic experience of her life. Her lower body clenched.

Again. Sound roared into her head, the thundering echo of her own heartbeat. He thrust. Her muscles clamped down on him, the pleasure so intense it bordered on pain.

"God. *Brent!*" Pleasure exploded, catapulting her into a climax so powerful, she screamed.

His fingers clenched on her waist. "Jen!" His hips drove once more, and he emptied himself with an exultant shout.

Jen wilted into an exhausted heap all over him.

He finally managed to get their clothes off, not that Jen helped much—it was a lot like stripping a Raggedy Ann doll. Brent didn't mind. If she was short on bones, he was the guy who'd wrung them out of her. Now she sprawled on top of him again, her face tucked against his neck. He had one arm wrapped around her waist to keep her close.

"Wild woman," Brent murmured fondly, and stroked a hand over her damp hair, inhaling the scents of flowers and Jen and sweat and sex.

"And don't you forget it, buster."

His hand swept down her back to pinch her butt.

"I'm not likely to, on account of you'll probably kill me before I'm forty."

"I'll probably kill both of us before we're forty. But at least we'll go with smiles on our faces."

"Yeah." He hugged a squeak out of her, then went back to stroking her hair. She felt so good, so absolutely right against him. And she loved him. He'd known it, of course, but he got a real kick out of hearing her say so. Got just as big a kick out of saying so himself. So he did. "I love you, honey."

She snuggled closer. "I love you too. It gets easier to say with practice, doesn't it? I sure had trouble getting it out the first time."

"You did all right."

"Because I had a plan."

She was so damned cute. "A plan, huh?"

He felt her nod. "Actually, it was Candy's idea. And it almost didn't work."

Tipping his head, he looked down at her. All he could make out was the sweep of hair across her cheek, one closed eye, and the leading edge of a satisfied smirk. "You talked to your friend about us? When was this?"

"Yesterday."

"Why'd you figure you needed her advice?"

"Well, I never told a man that I loved him before." While he basked in the glow of knowing he was the first, she continued, "Candy knows all about that kind of stuff; she's always falling in love."

"Oh, an expert. So what did she say?"

"She said I should put my arms around you, look deeply into your eyes, give you a long, juicy kiss, and tell you I love you."

He thought back. "And that's exactly what you did. I'll be damned."

"Probably," she agreed, and chuckled when he tugged on her hair. "Unfortunately, the plan had a major drawback. It didn't work at all the first time I tried it. Almost didn't work the second time."

"First time?"

"I tried to tell you when we were down on the beach. That's when I discovered the drawback."

"Oh." Remembering their lively encounter on the blanket, he felt himself start to harden again. "What drawback?"

"You'll get conceited."

That earned her a well-placed swat. "What was the drawback, woman?"

"The drawback," she said, brushing her lips against his neck, "is that I kiss you, and every single thought in my head vaporizes. If you can't think, you can't talk. If you can't talk, you can't say I love you. Get it?"

"Yeah." He paused, and grinned. "Vaporizes them, huh?"

"Don't sound so smug. Told you you'd get conceited."

"That is not conceit, that is justifiable manly pride."

"Proud of ourselves, are we?"

"What we are," he said in all seriousness, "is grateful. Very, very grateful."

Her head lifted, and she looked at him. "Grateful?"

"Yeah. If it hadn't been for you and your smart-ass letter, I'd still be a lonely social butterfly."

She scowled indignantly. "It wasn't a smart—social butterfly?"

"Hmm. When I read that article in *Celebrity*, I realized I was well on my way to boredom and uselessness. A damned social butterfly. Your letter more or less rubbed my nose in it, along with the noses of a couple million other people, of course, at which point I stopped being bored and became mad as hell. That being the case, I decided to pay you a little visit."

"You wanted revenge. Ugly, Brent, very ugly." She sighed and lay back down. "But I'm glad you did."

"Me too. Know why?"

She wriggled against his burgeoning erection. "I could probably make an educated guess."

"That, too, you shameless wench. But mostly I'm glad because when I found you I found everything I wanted, needed, and didn't have. Hell, I didn't even know there *were* things I didn't have until you came along. I just had to keep you with me long enough to figure out what they were."

"See there? What were they?"

"Oh, little things. Love. Pride. Self-respect. And really great sex, of course."

"Mmm. Those *are* good things."

"I had spaces when I met you, honey—big empty ones. You filled them up and made me happy again. I've got to thank you for that."

"Oh, Brent." Her arm slid around his neck. "That's the nicest thing anybody ever said to me. I love you so much."

"Love you, too, Jen." His fingers sifted through her hair. "Remember when you asked me what it was like to inherit all that money?"

"I remember. You said it was a surprise."

"It was that, all right. Like winning the lottery. It's taken me a while to figure it out, but winning the lottery can really screw up your life if you're not careful. Throws you off track, only you don't catch on right away, because you're too busy buying all those things you think will make you happy, like hot tubs and Porsches. It can get in your way and make you lose sight of the more important things."

Her fingers soothed the back of his neck. "Do you wish you'd never inherited?"

"No. I've been rich and I've been poor, and rich is definitely nicer. But it might have been better if I'd been older, made my own way for a while before my ship sailed in." He gave one creamy buttock an affectionate pat. "But now I've got you to keep me on my toes. Right?"

"Right. And I've got you to keep me from turning into a narrow-minded old-maid school teacher who looks down her nose at anybody different, and molders, and never tries anything new."

"So you're open to new experiences now, huh?"

"You bet."

"Does that mean you'll try calf's brains?"

"Not on your life."

He chuckled, and planted a kiss in her hair. For a while they lay quietly. But he was just biding his time, psyching himself up for his big move.

"So. Let's recap." He stretched. "We love each other. We also need each other. I need you to steer me along the straight and narrow, and you need me to drag you off it every once in a while. I can blow your mind with a kiss—"

"There you go getting conceited again."

"Absolutely. Now, where was I? Oh, yeah. I can blow your mind with a kiss and your lovemaking will kill us both before we're forty." He paused. "So are you going to marry me, or what?" His head had her answer calculated, but his heart hung in his throat.

She went still for a heartbeat, then lifted herself slightly, placing her hands on his chest. She set her chin on top of them. Lips pursed, she narrowed her eyes. "Well now, that depends."

Narrowed or not, her eyes were misty with love and happiness, and suddenly he was sure of her. He raised his eyebrows over the big, goofy smile that spread across his face. "On?"

"Are you going to take me up to some mountain-top in your helicopter?"

He remembered her letter to *Celebrity*, and his lips twitched. "Hell no," he drawled. "A very wise woman once told me that helicopter rides were the kiss of death as far as romance is concerned. Why? Do you *want* to go up in my helicopter?"

"Nuh-uh." She sighed dreamily. "But I'd kill for a ride on your Harley."

His chuckle rolled into a delighted laugh. "You've got it, baby. Anytime."

She grinned impishly. "Okay, you talked me into it. I'll marry you."

Sliding his hands into her hair, he held her for a quick, hard kiss. "Damn right you will," he said, and rolled on top of her to nestle between her thighs.

"Pretty sure of yourself, weren't you?" She ran her hands over his chest in a way guaranteed to get him hot and bothered in a hurry. "What would you have done if I'd said no?"

"Easy." He planted the next kiss between her breasts and slid his hand down to cup her. "I'd have made it a triple-dog dare."

She lifted into his touch with a long, satisfied sigh. "Oh, good. I never stood a chance."

THE EDITORS' CORNER

It's hot in the city! And in the country. And in the North. And in the South. And in the mountains. And at the seashore. And . . . well, you get the picture. It's just plain hot! Don't worry though, Loveswept's September loot of books will match the sultry weather out there. Even the air conditioner won't stop these characters from sizzling right off the pages and into your homes!

Devlin Sinclair and Gabrielle Rousseau are walking **ON THIN ICE**, LOVESWEPT #850, Eve Gaddy's novel about two attorneys bent on taking on the world and each other. Thrown together through no wish of their own, Devlin and Gabrielle must defend a reputed crime boss—a case that could ultimately make their careers, involving a man who could ultimately ruin Gabrielle's life. Devlin knew there was more to his sinfully gorgeous partner, especially since he accidentally bumped into her in the Midnight and Lace Lingerie shop! Annoyed that Devlin looked as if he'd guessed her wildest secrets, Gabrielle had to struggle not to melt when the charming rogue called her beautiful. But sometimes, in the heat of denial, one can discover heat of another kind. Eve Gaddy's romantic adventure pairs a fallen angel with a man who's her match in all things sensual and judicial!

In **AFTERGLOW**, LOVESWEPT #851 by Loveswept favorite Faye Hughes, professional treasure hunter Sean Kilpatrick is about to meet her match when she joins forces with Dalton Gregory in the search for a legendary cache of gold, silver, and priceless jewels buried somewhere on Gregory land. When Dalton comes to town to oust Sean, who he's sure is just a slick huckster on the make, he finds a copper-haired beauty whose enthusiasm for the project quickly becomes infectious. Sean is stunned by her intense attraction to this gorgeous, yet conservative history professor, but when he agrees to help chase a fortune, close quarters may not be all that they share. Spending more time together only accentuates the slow burn that is raging into a steady afterglow. Faye Hughes tempts readers with the ultimate treasure hunt in a tantalizingly steamy romantic romp!

Cheryln Biggs tells a deliciously unpredictable tale about the **GUNSLINGER'S LADY**, LOVE-SWEPT #852. There's a new girl in town in Tombstone, Arizona, and Jack Ringo aims to find out just what she's doing sprawled in his cactus patch dressed up in petticoats—especially since the Old West Festival doesn't start until tomorrow! Kate Holliday can't understand why Johnny Ringo is dressed up in strange clothes and without his guns, but the man was definitely as dangerously handsome as ever! Jack is quickly bewitched by Kate's mystery, frustrated at her existence, and inflamed by the heated passion of a woman who may disappear with the dawn. Adrift in a world she'd never imagined, uncertain of all but one man's need, can a sassy adventuress find her future in the arms of a man who couldn't guarantee the coming of tomorrow? Cheryln Biggs delivers a timeless love story that dabbles in destiny and breaks all the rules!

Loveswept newcomer Pat Van Wie adds to our lineup of delectable September romances **RUNNING FOR COVER**, LOVESWEPT #853. When Deputy Marshal Kyle Munroe shows up at Jennifer Brooks's classroom door complete with an entourage, Jenny knows that her time of peace and security is long gone. Jenny is reluctant to trust the man who had once shunned all she had to offer, but deep down she knows that Kyle may very well be the only one she can truly count on. Threats against her father's life also put hers in danger and the reluctant pair go into hiding . . . until betrayal catapults them into a desperate flight. And once again, Kyle and Jenny are faced with the same decisions, whether to find safety and love together, or shadows and sadness apart. Sizzling with sexual tension and the breathless thrill of love on the run, Pat Van Wie's first Loveswept explores the joy and heartache of a desire too strong to subdue.

Happy reading!

With warmest regards,

Shauna Summers *Joy Abella*

Shauna Summers   Joy Abella

Editor   Administrative Editor

P.S. Look for these Bantam women's fiction titles coming in August. *New York Times* bestseller Tami Hoag's breathtakingly sensual novel, **DARK PARADISE**, is filled with heart-stopping suspense and shocking passion. Marilee Jennings is drawn to a man as hard and untamable as the land he loves, and to a town steeped in secrets—where a killer lurks. Another *New York Times* bestselling author, Betina Krahn, is back with **THE MERMAID,** a tale of a woman ahead of her time and an academic who must decide if he will risk everything he holds dear to side with the Lady Mermaid. Dubbed the queen of romantic adventure by *Affaire de Coeur*, Katherine O'Neal returns with **BRIDE OF DANGER,** her most spellbinding—and irresistible—novel yet! Night after night, Mylene charmed the secrets out of men's souls, and not one suspected that she was a spy devoted to the cause of freedom. Until the evening she came face-to-face with the mysterious Lord Whitney, a man who will ask her to betray everything she's ever believed in. And immediately following this page, preview the Bantam women's fiction titles on sale in July.

Don't miss these extraordinary books
by your favorite Bantam authors

On sale in July:

THE SILVER ROSE
by Jane Feather

A PLACE TO CALL HOME
by Deborah Smith

The newest novel in the enthralling,
passionate Charm Bracelet Trilogy . . .

"Jane Feather is an accomplished
storyteller . . . rare and wonderful."
—*Daily News of Los Angeles*

THE SILVER ROSE
by Jane Feather
author of *The Diamond Slipper*

*Like the rose in the haunting tale of "Beauty and the
Beast," a silver rose on a charm bracelet brings together a
young woman and a battle-scarred lord . . . Ariel
Ravenspeare has been taught to loathe the earl of
Hawkesmoor and everything he represents. Their two
families have been sworn enemies for generations. But it's
one thing to hate him, and another to play the part
her vicious brothers have written for her—trapping
Hawkesmoor into a marriage that will destroy him, using
herself as bait. Forced into the marriage, Ariel will find
her new husband unexpectedly difficult to manipulate, as
well as surprisingly—and powerfully—attractive. But
beneath the passion lurks the strand of a long-hidden
secret . . . a secret embodied in a sparkling silver rose.*

Ranulf stood at the door to the Great Hall. He stared
out over the thronged courtyard, and when he saw
Ariel appear from the direction of the stables, he de-

scended the steps and moved purposefully toward her. She was weaving her way through the crowd, the dogs at her heels, a preoccupied frown on her face.

"Just where the hell have you been?" Ranulf demanded in a low voice, grabbing her arm above the elbow. The dogs growled but for once he ignored them. "How dare you vanish without a word to anyone! Where have you been? Answer me!" He shook her arm. The dogs growled again, a deep-throated warning. Ranulf turned on them with a foul oath, but he released his hold.

"Why should it matter where I've been?" Ariel answered. "I'm back now."

"Dressed like some homespun peasant's wife," her brother gritted through compressed lips. "Look at you. You had money to clothe yourself properly for your bridal celebrations, and you go around in an old riding habit that looks as if it's been dragged through a haystack. And your boots are worn through."

Ariel glanced down at her broadcloth skirts. Straw and mud clung to them, and her boots, while not exactly worn through, were certainly shabby and unpolished. She had been so uncomfortable dressing under the amused eye of her bridegroom that morning that she had grabbed what came to hand and given no thought to the occasion.

"I trust you have passed a pleasant morning, my wife." Simon's easy tones broke into Ranulf's renewed diatribe. The earl of Hawkesmoor had approached through the crowd so quietly that neither Ranulf nor his sister had noticed him. Ariel looked up with a flashing smile that betrayed her relief at his interruption.

"I went for a drive in the gig. Forgive me for

staying out overlong, but I drove farther than I'd thought to without noticing the time."

"Aye, it's a fine way to do honor to your husband," Ranulf snapped. "To appear clad like a serving wench who's been rolling in the hay. I'll not have it said that the earl of Ravenspeare's sister goes about like a tavern doxy—"

"Oh, come now, Ravenspeare!" Simon again interrupted Ranulf's rising tirade. "You do even less honor to your name by reviling your sister so publicly." Ariel flushed to the roots of her hair, more embarrassed by her husband's defense than by her brother's castigation.

"Your wife's appearance does not reflect upon the Hawkesmoor name, then?" Ranulf's tone was full of sardonic mockery. "But perhaps Hawkesmoors are less nice in their standards."

"From what I've seen of your hospitality so far, Ravenspeare, I take leave to doubt that," Simon responded smoothly, not a flicker of emotion in his eyes. He turned to Ariel, who was still standing beside him, wrestling with anger and chagrin. "However, I take your point, Ravenspeare. It is for a husband to correct his wife, not her brother.

"You are perhaps a little untidy, my dear. Maybe you should settle this matter by changing into a habit that will reflect well upon both our houses. I am certain the shooting party can wait a few minutes."

Ariel turned and left without a word. She kept her head lowered, her hood drawn up to hide her scarlet cheeks. It was one of her most tormenting weaknesses. Her skin was so fair and all her life she had blushed at the slightest provocation, sometimes even without good reason. She was always mortified at her obvious embarrassment, and the situation would be impossibly magnified.

Why had Simon interfered? Ranulf's insulting rebukes ran off her like water on oiled leather. By seeming to take her part, the Hawkesmoor had made a mountain out of a molehill. But then, he hadn't really taken her part. He had sent her away to change as if she were a grubby child appearing unwashed at the dinner table.

However, when she took a look at herself in the glass in her chamber, she was forced to admit that both men had had a point. Her hair was a wind-whipped tangle, her face was smudged with dust from her drive through the Fen blow, and her old broadcloth riding habit was thick with dust, the skirts caked with mud. But she'd had more important matters to attend to than her appearance, she muttered crossly, tugging at buttons and hooks.

Clad in just her shift, she washed her face and sponged her arms and neck, before letting down her hair. Throwing it forward over her face, she bent her head low and began to brush out the tangles. She was still muttering to herself behind the honeyed curtain when her husband spoke from the door.

"Your brothers' guests grow restless. I don't have much skill as a ladies' maid but perhaps I can help you."

Ariel raised her head abruptly, tossing back the glowing mane of hair. Her cheeks were pink with her efforts with the hairbrush and a renewed surge of annoyance.

The hounds greeted the new arrival with thumping tails. Their mistress, however, regarded the earl with a fulminating glare. "I have no need of assistance, my lord. And it's very discourteous to barge into my chamber without so much as a knock."

"Forgive me, but the door was ajar." His tone carelessly dismissed her objection. He closed the door on his words and surveyed her with his crooked little smile. "Besides, a wife's bedchamber is usually not barred to her husband."

"So you've already made clear, my lord," Ariel said tightly. "And I suppose it follows that a wife has no rights to privacy."

"Not necessarily." He limped forward and took the brush from her hand. "Sit." A hand on her shoulder pushed her down to the dresser stool. He began to draw the brush through the thick springy locks with strong, rhythmic strokes. "I've longed to do this since I saw you yesterday, waiting for me in the courtyard, with your hat under your arm. The sun was catching these light gold streaks in your hair. They're quite delightful." He lifted a strand that stood out much paler against the rich dark honey.

Ariel glanced at his face in the mirror. He was smiling to himself, his eyes filled with a sensual pleasure, his face, riven by the jagged scar, somehow softened as if this hair brushing were the act of a lover. She noticed how his hands, large and callused though they were, had an elegance, almost a delicacy to them. She had the urge to reach for those hands, to lay her cheek against them. A shiver ran through her.

"You're cold," he said immediately, laying down the brush. "The fire is dying." He turned to the hearth and with deft efficiency poked it back to blazing life, throwing on fresh logs. "Come now, you must make haste with your dressing before you catch cold." He limped to the armoire. "Will you wear the habit you wore yesterday? The crimson velvet suited you well." He drew out the garment as he spoke, and looked over at the sparse contents of the armoire. "You appear to have a very limited wardrobe, Ariel."

"I have little need of finery in the Fens," she stated, almost snatching the habit from him. "The life I lead doesn't lend itself to silks and velvets."

"The life you've led until now," he corrected thoughtfully, leaning against the bedpost, arms folded, as he watched her dress. "As the countess of Hawkesmoor, you will take your place at court, and in county society, I trust. The Hawkesmoors have always been active in our community of the Fens."

Unlike the lords of Ravenspeare. The local community was more inclined to hide from them than seek their aid. But neither of them spoke this shared thought.

Ariel fumbled with the tiny pearl buttons of her shirt. Her fingers were suddenly all thumbs. He sounded so assured, but she knew that she would never take her place at court or anywhere else as the wife of this man, whatever happened.

"Your hands must be freezing." He moved her fumbling fingers aside and began to slip the tiny buttons into the braided loops that fastened them. His hands brushed her breasts and her breath caught. His fingers stopped their work and she felt her nipples harden against the fine linen of her shift as goose bumps lifted on her skin. Then abruptly his hands dropped from her and he stepped back, his face suddenly closed.

She turned aside to pick up her skirt, stepping into it, fastening the hooks at her waist, trying to hide the trembling of her fingers, keeping her head lowered and averted until the hot flush died down on her creamy cheeks.

If only he would go away now. But he remained leaning against the bedpost.

She felt his eyes on her, following her every move, and that lingering sensuality in his gaze made her blood race. Even the simple act of pulling on her boots was invested with a curious voluptuousness under the intentness of his sea blue eyes. The man was ugly as sin, and yet she had never felt more powerfully attracted to anyone.

A new novel from one of the most
appealing voices in Southern fiction . . .

"A uniquely significant voice in contemporary
women's fiction."
—*Romantic Times*

A PLACE TO CALL HOME

by Deborah Smith

author of *Silk and Stone*

*Deborah Smith offers an irresistible Southern saga that
celebrates a sprawling, sometimes eccentric Georgia family
and the daughter at the center of their hearts. Twenty
years ago, Claire Maloney was the willful, pampered child
of the town's most respected family, but that didn't stop her
from befriending Roan Sullivan, a fierce, motherless boy
who lived in a rusted-out trailer amid junked cars. No
one in Dunderry—least of all Claire's family—could
understand the attraction. But Roan and Claire belonged
together . . . until the dark afternoon when violence and
terror overtook them and Roan disappeared from Claire's
life. Now, two decades later, Claire is adrift and the
Maloneys are still hoping the past can be buried under the
rich Southern soil . . .*

I planned to be the kind of old Southern lady who talks to her tomato plants and buys sweaters for her cats. I'd just turned thirty, but I was already sizing up where I'd been and where I was headed. So I knew that when I was old I'd be deliberately *peculiar*. I'd wear bright red lipstick and tell embarrassing true stories about my family, and people would say, "I heard she was always a little funny, if you know what I mean."

They wouldn't understand why, and I didn't intend to tell them. I thought I'd sit in a rocking chair on the porch of some fake-antebellum nursing home for decrepit journalists, get drunk on bourbon and Coca-Cola, and cry over Roan Sullivan. I was only ten the last time I saw him, and he was fifteen, and twenty years had passed since then, but I'd never forgotten him and knew I never would.

"I'd like to believe life turned out well for Roanie," Mama said periodically, and Daddy nodded without meeting her eyes, and they dropped the subject. They felt guilty about the part they'd played in driving Roan away, and they knew I couldn't forgive them for it. He was one of the disappointments between them and me, which was saying a lot, since I'd felt like such a helpless failure when they brought me home from the hospital last spring.

My two oldest brothers, Josh and Brady, didn't speak about Roan at all. They were away at college during most of the Roan Sullivan era in our family. But my two other brothers remembered him each time they came back from a hunting trip with a prize buck. "It can't hold a candle to the one Roan Sullivan shot when we were kids," Evan always said to Hop. "Nope," Hop agreed with a mournful sigh. "That buck was a king." Evan and Hop measured regret in terms of antlers.

As for the rest of the family—Daddy's side, Mama's side, merged halves of a family tree so large and complex and deeply rooted it looked like an overgrown oak to strangers—Roan Sullivan was only a fading reflection in the mirror of their biases and regrets and sympathies. How they remembered him depended on how they saw themselves and our world back then, and most of them had turned that painful memory to the wall.

But he and I were a permanent fixture in local history, as vivid and tragic as anything could be in a small Georgia community isolated in the lap of the mountains, where people hoard sad stories as carefully as their great-grandmothers' china. My great-grandmother's glassware and china service, by the way, were packed in a crate in Mama and Daddy's attic. Mama had this wistful little hope that I'd use it someday, that her only girl among five children would magically and belatedly blossom into the kind of woman who set a table with china instead of plastic.

There was hope for that. But what happened to Roan Sullivan and me changed my life and changed my family. Because of him we saw ourselves as we were, made of the kindness and cruelty that bond people together by blood, marriage, and time. I tried to save him and he ended up saving me. He might have been dead for twenty years—I didn't know then—but I knew I'd come full circle because of him: I would always wait for him to come back, too.

The hardest memories are the pieces of what might have been.

On sale in August:

DARK PARADISE
by Tami Hoag

THE MERMAID
by Betina Krahn

BRIDE OF DANGER
by Katherine O'Neal

The enchanting wit of *New York Times* bestseller

Betina Krahn

"Krahn has a delightful, smart touch."
—*Publishers Weekly*

The Perfect Mistress
___56523-0 $5.99/$7.99 Canada

The Last Bachelor
___56522-2 $5.99/$7.50 Canada

The Unlikely Angel
___56524-9 $5.99/$7.99 Canada